Dream Racer

Dream Racer

*Side Streets series—
standalone reads*

Jacqueline Guest

James Lorimer & Company Ltd., Publishers
Toronto

FIC
GUE

James Lorimer & Company Ltd. acknowledges the support of the Ontario Arts Council. We acknowledge the support of the Government of Canada through the Book Publishing Industry Development Program (BPIDP) for our publishing activities. We acknowledge the support of the Canada Council for the Arts for our publishing program. We acknowledge the support of the Government of Ontario through the Ontario Media Development Corporation's Ontario Book Initiative.

The Canada Council | Le Conseil des Arts
for the Arts | du Canada

ONTARIO ARTS COUNCIL
CONSEIL DES ARTS DE L'ONTARIO

Cover design: Clarke MacDonald

Library and Archives Canada Cataloguing in Publication

Guest, Jacqueline

Dream racer / Jacqueline Guest. (SideStreets)

ISBN 10 1-55028-945-4 (bound)

ISBN 13 978-1-55028-945-9 (bound)

ISBN 10 1-55028-942-X (pbk.)

ISBN 13 978-1-55028-942-8 (pbk.)

     I. Title. II. Series

PS8563.U365D74 2006   jC813'.54   C2006-903649-7

James Lorimer
& Company Ltd., Publishers
317 Adelaide St. W., Suite 1002
Toronto, Ontario
M5V 1P9
www.lorimer.ca

Distributed in the
U.S. by:
Orca Book Publishers
P.O. Box 468
Custer, WA USA
98240-0468

Printed and bound in Canada

For Gordon,
who understands racing after a dream.

Chapter 1

The car rocketed into the corner and leaned over hard on the sagging suspension as Zoë Kendall fought for control. Jerking the wheel back, she narrowly avoided a woman pushing a toddler in a stroller as the car careened to the other side of the narrow cobblestone street.

Zoë knew she was quickly running out of options.

Without warning, a towering bridge abutment loomed into view directly in her path. The road disappeared into the black shadows under the bridge leaving Zoë with no clue as to what waited on the other side.

"Just friggin' great!" Zoë groaned as she manoeuvred between the mammoth steel pylons, but it was like squeezing toothpaste back into the tube. The big car spread out to fill the entire road. The alley was way too narrow for the hulking tank she was driving. If she could get the vehicle straightened out, she still had a slim chance of making the opening.

Cursing, Zoë shifted down. The engine screamed as the car abruptly slowed, but the wheels continued on their suicidal course.

With a desperate effort, she managed to pull the car into line, a split second before a quick movement in her peripheral vision made her jerk her head around. A small black Scottie dog scurried into her path, unaware of the deadly missile hurtling toward it.

Zoë had no choice. It was her or the pooch and she'd always liked Scotties.

Cranking the wheel hard over, she pointed the car directly at the steel stanchion and smiled as her car smashed into it head-on.

"What the hell did you do that for?"

Zoë looked up into her boyfriend's questioning face and frowned. "Because, this beast deserved to die an ugly death. The next time we play arcade racing, I get to pick the car *you* drive, Adam Harlow!" She clambered out of the seat of the video game.

"It understeers like a pig, has marshmallow suspension, weighs as much as an aircraft carrier and is two lanes wide!"

"Fine with me! I can drive anything you can build." Adam grinned impishly, then crossed his arms. "But you have to admit, you're in a much better mood than when we walked in here."

"So that was your evil master plan. Whisk me away after school to this den of iniquity …" she tipped her head at the laughing, noisy kids playing video games, "then dial up a real bear of a car and let me take my frustration out on some virtual four-wheeled slug."

Adam draped his arm around her shoulders and gave her a quick kiss. "Pretty much. Now, let's get something to eat before I take you home."

His kiss left her lips tingling. There was no denying it: Zoë loved being with this guy. He knew exactly how to make her forget the rest of the world and concentrate on theirs.

And he'd been right. Zoë's black mood after arguing with her mother earlier that day had been forgotten, but now she felt her spirits sag again. Most days, her mom was the best person on the planet, but Zoë's older brother Trent had pushed her to the wall again, and the fallout was affecting their mother–daughter relationship.

Zoë hated to see her mom so bummed, especially after all her parents had been through with Trent, who had *problems*, big time. Not only was he a poster child for ADHD, attention deficit hyperactivity disorder, he'd also been in a serious car accident that left him with a permanent limp and a scarred face. A freshman at McGill University, he'd been doing okay for a while, but now seemed to be totally flunking out.

On more than one occasion, Zoë had heard her parents arguing about what to do with dear little

Trent. For crying out loud, he was a big boy, why didn't they cut the cord? The stress was making her mom age right before Zoë's eyes. But that was still no reason for her mother to do what she had done.

Zoë took Adam's hand and led him through the crowded arcade to a pizza cart near the exit. "Pizza will do fine, hotshot. I'm not really hungry. Besides, my mom has some fancy dinner arranged later with some old fogey and I'll have to do the good little daughter thing and eat then."

Adam gave her a suspicious look. "How *not really hungry* are you, one piece or two?"

Zoë laughed. In the year they'd been dating, she'd developed the habit of snacking off his plate or snagging a bite of his burger. She honestly never seemed to have an appetite until Adam's food arrived, then she turned into some kind of starving refugee. He'd long ago wised up to her and now it was a joke between them.

"Mmm," she wrinkled her nose as she decided. "I think two will do."

"And I suppose you're not thirsty either?" he asked, raising an eyebrow.

"Maybe a smidge." She held up two fingers barely a millimetre apart. "Hey, I'm a healthy seventeen-year-old girl. I need to keep up my strength."

"Keep your strength up any more, and you might be an unhealthy seventeen-year-old girl."

He eyed her as though assessing whether the pizza had already added inches to her hips, so Zoë wiggled her equipment provocatively. At nearly five-foot-ten, she'd always been on the thin side, and eating wasn't something she worried about … too much. She liked her lithe body and knew she looked good walking down the hall at school.

Zoë found a booth while Adam went for their food. She watched as he juggled the tray heaped with hot pizza and cold pops. When he slid in next to her, he purposely bumped his hip against hers and this made Zoë feel great. It was cool to know he wanted to show the world they were a couple.

Adam quickly finished his snack. "I am stoked about watching the Paris-Dakar rally this week-end. My dad put a rush on the cable guy, so we can get the new satellite feed live and see the actual finish of the race from the comfort of our living room." He leaned in and nuzzled Zoë's neck. "We'll have to pull a dusk-to-dawn to watch it. Do you think your parents will object to your spending the night with me?" he whispered, as his tongue danced in her ear.

Zoë shivered at the pleasant sensation, then turned to face him. "Both your parents will be there, and so will four other guys from the Calgary Sports Car Club. It will hardly be a love nest."

"Yeah, I suppose, but a guy can fantasize can't he? Besides, it will give us a chance to talk about strategy for our own big race, which, by the way, is coming up way too quickly. We've been planning for the High Mountain Run for so long, I can't believe it's only two weeks away. That race is going to be a blast, Zoë. A twisty mountain road, you behind the wheel of a fast rally car, and me sitting a gear shift away. Ah, heaven wrapped up in one extreme package!" He rolled his eyes heavenward.

At the mention of the rally, Zoë felt her stress level ramp up a notch, but didn't flinch. Adam was such a great guy, she hated the thought of what was coming.

"I'm keeping my fingers crossed that trick suspension you designed will make it in time," he continued, "but we should have a fallback plan in case Gruber and Gruber, fabricator to the stars, screws up. Man, the world of automotive design will never be the same once Zoë Kendall, engineer extraordinaire, comes on stream."

Zoë tugged at the lock of her short auburn hair Adam's snuggling had messed up. "Yeah, in the past, engineering seemed to be a fit, but who knows? Maybe I'm really meant to be a rocket scientist."

"Right, or a brain surgeon!" He grinned. "Engineering is one life choice you never have to think twice about, Zoë, trust me on that one."

Zoë didn't want to think about *life choices* right now. She didn't want to talk about the rally they were entered in either, not after her conversation with her mom.

How could she tell Adam that her mother saw her life heading in a totally different direction — one that didn't include cars, rallying, and perhaps not even him?

She stared at her pizza, eyes unfocused.

Zoë remembered when her dad had bought his first rally car. She'd been just a little girl, but had instantly fallen in love with the speed and skill that went into the sport. She also liked the fact that you didn't have to be a millionaire to rally. Any car worked if it met the safety specs, had a roll cage, and could take the pounding as it was driven at full speed down some wilderness goat track that passed for a road.

Of course, it didn't mean you'd win without throwing some cash at your ride, but the heart-pounding adrenaline rush that came from rallying could happen at any speed.

When Trent became involved in the sport, it had turned into a real Kendall family thing, except for their mom, who'd never liked it. Zoë had wanted to drive since she was too small to reach the clutch pedal and her dad had fixed a wooden block to it so she could shift gears.

Now she was their team's one and only driver in Adam's re-tuned '95 Honda Civic. He was the co-driver, the navigator, who directed her when to turn and what to expect on the fast-twisting mountain roads they rallied on.

It was this passion that had led to her secret dream of designing cars — perfect, beautiful cars that purred down the highway. At least it *had been* her dream …

She shook herself back into the present and, reached for the steaming slice, pulled her hand back, her appetite suddenly evaporating. Adam didn't seem to notice her change of mood.

"I'm telling you Zoë, when we go to the University of Ontario, they are getting two fine students. Your design ideas will set that new automotive engineering school right on their asses, and me, well I've got some pretty rad moves of my own lined up for electrical engineering." He motioned to her untouched portion. "Don't you want that?"

Zoë shook her head. "I think I'll skip the gourmet meal."

"You okay, Bunny? It's not like you to pass on *my* food."

Zoë smiled at the use of his silly pet name for her and nodded as though everything was normal and she didn't feel sick.

"Okay, don't say you didn't have your chance."

She watched him polish off the last piece, then before he could make another totally distracting move on her, Zoë grabbed her hoodie and slid out of the booth. "I've got to go."

Adam seemed a little taken aback at her haste but nodded, took a gulp of his drink, then stood and held out his hand to her. "Your wish is my command, my lady."

Zoë felt like a first-class loser crossed with a low-life coward. She had to tell Adam what was going on, but not now, she hated making a scene in public.

Chapter 2

Zoë parked her bright yellow '97 Mitsubishi Eclipse in the driveway. She considered the car her baby, and patted the hood affectionately before going into the house. The Kendall home was palatial. Her parents were what her mother called "people of influence," and it showed.

The front door had barely closed behind her when she heard her mother calling.

"Zoë honey, can you come into the study for a minute? We need to talk."

With a sigh, Zoë steeled herself for whatever new calamity was coming. "I'll be there in a minute, Mom. I'm putting my books away." She took her time going upstairs, then down the thickly carpeted hallway to her bedroom. Whatever was on her mother's mind, Zoë didn't want to hear it.

Her mom was into the bonding thing lately, and

it was a little freaky. Strike that, Zoë corrected, a *lot* freaky. Did her mother really think they were going to become best buddies? Okay, if she were being honest with herself, she had to admit it wasn't really so terrible. Zoë wanted her mom in her corner, and if it meant sharing a glass of milk and a couple of cookies, so what? She owed her mom that. And it was cool to have someone older, with a thousand years of experience, to talk to. Especially when you were feeling in over your head. It was like having a safety valve on a pressure cooker.

The only problem was her mother thought their new closer relationship gave her carte blanche to steer her daughter's life in whatever direction she thought was the right. It was like Zoë suddenly had a private handler who took the worry out of thinking for herself.

That's what the fight this morning had been about. Her mother had dropped the bomb that she was going ahead with "their" plans to get Zoë into the University of Calgary, first for her undergrad in biological sciences, then on to medical school!

Zoë had said medicine wasn't her plan at all, and that she'd decide a career direction for herself when the time came. Things had sort of gone downhill from there. She'd left by banging the front door closed so hard the expensive Italian stained glass had rattled ominously.

Zoë took a deep breath and exhaled, then walked into the richly furnished study, where she found her mother reading a letter at the large oak desk. The room was warm and inviting, with ornate carpets and tall floor-to-ceiling bookcases. Opposite these were windows overlooking a flagstone patio and the expansive backyard.

Her mother was not happy. The corners of her mouth were set in that way that let Zoë know there was trouble in paradise. She hastily put the letter to the side of the desk as Zoë, auto-smile plastered to her face, walked over.

"What's up, Mom?" Zoë asked brightly, noting the McGill logo on the abandoned letter.

"Have a seat, honey." Her mother motioned to one of the overstuffed leather chairs next to the desk.

Laura Kendall was all about being a young society matron. Her highlighted blonde hair was perfectly coifed, and with her expertly applied makeup, she didn't appear anywhere near old enough to be Zoë's mother.

Flopping down heavily, Zoë stretched her legs out haphazardly and dangled her arms limply over the sides of the chair.

Her mother gave the "guilt tilt" with her head. "Honestly, Zoë, you look like a cadaver in free fall."

Grimacing, Zoë sat up straighter.

"About this morning ..." her mom hesitated. "I may have been a little overzealous in my ideas, but I only want what's best for you, sweetheart. Previously, you've had some problems with focus and with making wise choices. I don't want you to repeat your brother's pattern."

Zoë groaned inwardly. It was worse than she'd thought. Her past was back to bite her. "Mom, I know I haven't exactly been a model student, or daughter either, for that matter, but that's ancient history. Can we forget my misspent youth and focus on now?"

Her mother's back stiffened. "I'm trying to have an adult conversation with you. Please try to stay with me."

Zoë wanted to tell her mom she was the one who was about to open the book of old sins again, but instead she bit back the words. Her mom was right. She'd been heading for a train wreck, but when Adam had come back into her life, things became different. She'd changed.

Adam had needed a driver for his '95 Civic with a fast JDM engine, and Zoë had been a natural choice. As a team, they were good, and that partnership spilled over into other parts of their lives.

They'd become best friends, and then more, confiding their dreams for the future and laughing when it turned out they both wanted to go to the University of Ontario.

Zoë had talked about enrolling in the new Automotive Centre of Excellence Program with its high-tech, state-of-the-art car design and engineering tools. It was off the chart on the wow-factor scale.

When he finished his electrical engineering

degree, Adam wanted to work on electronic component design for high performance cars.

They fit together like hand and glove, popcorn and butter, hot and tub — well, she knew what she meant.

Zoë had shared none of these dreams with her parents. In the past, her plans for the future had changed as regularly as the colour of her lip gloss. She'd wanted to be everything from an actress to a zookeeper, but there'd always been cars in there somewhere. Trying to explain how she felt about cars to her mom was out of the question. She'd only think Zoë was off on one of her short-lived career-of-the-week things.

Fighting long, drawn-out, endless battles wasn't one of Zoë's strong points. Nope, she knew when to throw in the towel.

"Sorry, I was out of line," Zoë began. "I know you want me to succeed ..."

Her mother cut her off. "Exactly, and we both know you haven't really had your eye on the brass ring for the past year." Her tone grew hard again. "I knew as soon as you started rallying with Adam Harlow that everything else would take a back seat to that damn car. I don't know what's the matter with this family. Everyone except me seems to be obsessed with cars!"

Zoë really hoped her mom wasn't going to launch into one of her tirades on how the devil drove a fast car, and rallying would get you a one-way ticket to hell. That had become lame a long time ago after Trent had totalled his car. Her mother went on without missing a beat.

"It's time for you to figure out what you're going to do with the rest of your life, Zoë, and as far as I can discern, you have no more idea about that than you would about flying to the moon."

Her mom was not one for leaving empty spaces unfilled, and lately that included Zoë's future. Wild Child Zoë had never hinted she wanted to do more than coast after high school, but Engineer Zoë did have a game plan, sort of. Her dad didn't seem to mind that his little girl could end up in some steady, but maybe a tad tedious nine-to-five job, but her mom had other ideas. Maybe now was the time to clear things up.

"I've been thinking about it, honest. In fact, there's this new program where I could actually design race cars …"

Her mother slammed her fist down on the table so hard that Zoë jumped. *"Design cars!* That's the most ridiculous thing I've ever heard!" She stood up and paced the room, her agitation like electricity in the air. "Cars are nothing but a way to waste time. When I think of how rallying has stolen so much away from your father and me while he travelled everywhere with those bloody cars of his! If he'd spent more time at home with his family, especially you and Trent, maybe life would be more normal around here."

Zoë was getting a little nervous. She'd never seen her mom so wound up before.

"Have you forgotten your brother's accident?" she went on. "Do you think if he hadn't had his head filled with all that rally nonsense, he might not have ended up in a burning car at the bottom of a cliff?"

Zoë felt her own temper rising.

"So what you're saying is, in short: cars are the root of all evil, and medicine would be my salvation. End of story. And as for Trent, he always got to do whatever he wanted, and driving like a maniac was one of the things he did, Mom. You and Dad always cut him way more slack than you did me!"

"That's not true and you know it! Your father indulged you every chance he got. He's the one who first got you driving those, those ..."

Her mother looked like she was about to really lose it, and Zoë cringed.

"*Cars!*" her mother exploded, "You got away with things no other teenager would have been allowed to do." Steam was practically coming out of her ears. "Would you like me to list a few of your escapades, young lady?"

Zoë's face flushed. She knew that list and it was a long one, but come on ... what kid didn't mess up now and then? "Okay, so I screwed up big time in the past, but that's just it, Mom, *in the past*. I was way young then, and trying to prove some dumb point, but I'm not like that now."

Her mother closed her eyes for a moment as though waiting for the anger to dissipate, then came over to sit in the chair beside her daughter's.

"Honey, all I'm saying is you have to think about this rationally. You have a future with promise and I know you want your life to mean something. Medicine is a fine career, one you can be proud of."

Zoë saw the love in her mother's eyes. It was hard to argue with that. And Zoë hadn't actually done anything to make her future as an engineer happen. Her mom was right on that one. Coasting wasn't just a bad habit with Zoë — it was a way of life.

Sighing, her mom got up and walked to the window.

Zoë felt her own anger evaporate. Maybe her dream of designing cars was simply a way of never having to grow up and leave behind rallying and having fun every weekend. She remembered reading about the "Peter Pan Syndrome" where people didn't want the responsibility of growing up and did things to sabotage their success as adults. Was that what she was doing by wanting to design cars?

And Zoë also knew her mom's fast-tracking the U of C program was only one ring in the Kendall Family Circus. There was Trent and his ongoing gong show, which always provided tension and drama in the house.

Then the problems got truly serious. A disaster was looming that was bigger than either Zoë or her brother. Things between her dad and mom were not going well. In fact, Zoë was deathly afraid they were terminal. She'd had enough friends whose parents were divorced that she could recognize the signs.

Her dad was a high-powered lawyer with political aspirations that he hoped would one day lead him to the big chair on Parliament Hill. Currently, he was running for member of parliament for their constituency.

Her mother thought the price was too high — his being away from home a lot more, his time and energy used up so that there was none left for his own family, their plans for retirement postponed. She adamantly opposed the new game plan. They hardly spoke to one another anymore, and when they did, the knives came out.

He'd moved into one of the spare rooms, and in a house the size of the Kendall's, that was like being a subcontinent away. Her parents made up excuses why they weren't sleeping together, something about his loud snoring, but come on, Zoë wasn't stupid.

Her mother turned back to her. "Honey, do you understand what I've been trying to say, and why I want this so badly for you?"

Zoë's attention refocused with a bang. "Not really, Mom."

"When I was your age, I had dreams too. They were shelved when my babies came along. In our home, a wife's first duty was to her family and, of course, the idea of me leaving two small children while I pursued a career ... well, it simply wasn't done. You, however, have a wonderful opportunity to make this dream come true." She sat beside Zoë again and took her daughter's hands in hers. "Zoë, darling, I'm convinced — *you could be a doctor*! All it would take is to knuckle down and concentrate. Medical school is a worthy goal, Zoë. I don't want you looking back when you're fifty and feeling like you've wasted your life."

Zoë had heard this speech before, but hadn't paid much attention. Mothers were always going on about this for their daughters or that for their sons. Before today, Zoë had found smiling and nodding while she listened to her iPod at max volume was the best way to handle the whole thing.

"I have an old sorority sister from Delta Kappa Phi coming to dinner tonight. She teaches at the U of C's faculty of medicine, and I thought it would be a great time for you to introduce yourself. I think knowing her would do you a lot of good when you begin your pre-med. You could consider this lady your personal faculty advisor." She smiled at her daughter.

Zoë sat up. "You mean the old fogey is coming to talk to me!" Her voice rose. This was now officially out of hand. She had to get this thing straightened out or she'd be knee deep in bedpans before she knew what hit her. Zoë tried frantically to remember if she had actually agreed to anything. Was nodding and smiling insanely some kind of silent agreement that would hold up in a court of law?

Her mom stood and paced the room again. "I know this seems sudden, dear, but I've been giving it a lot of thought and time is passing us by." She turned to Zoë. "Honey, you like to let things slide, sometimes to the point where opportunities slip through your fingers, and are lost forever. I thought I would help out this time, make sure that doesn't happen. I've taken some steps …"

She had Zoë's full attention now. "What steps?"

Before her mother could answer, the doorbell rang. "Oh, that must be Fatima. Hurry and change dear." She bustled out of the study as Zoë sat in a state of shock. Things were totally out of control.

Chapter 3

Zoë slowly stood to leave. Out of the corner of her eye, the letter her mother had been reading caught her attention. She picked it up and scanned the short message.

Great! Trent, the *idiot savant*, with an emphasis on the *idiot*, had done it again. He'd cut so many classes he was now on probation. One more screw-up and he was kicked out of school. Being skidded by McGill would look friggin' wonderful on his resume!

This was all her mother needed. No wonder she'd been out of control with Zoë.

Her mom had been so happy when Trent had received his chemistry scholarship last year; she could have done an ad for Prozac. That had been a bright spot in the Kendall house, but it hadn't lasted. And now, with her parents' constant tension and bickering remarks, life at home had gone to hell.

Zoë dropped the letter like it was covered in acid, then left to get changed.

She was still debating what to wear when there was a knock on the bedroom door.

"I'm not quite ready yet," Zoë called.

"Maybe I can help." Her mom came in, saw Zoë's unchanged state, and went straight to the closet. She leafed through her daughter's dresses, then held up a frilly, sickly green one Zoë's grandmother had sent two Christmases ago.

Zoë's eyebrows shot up.

Her mother held out the long, full skirt, then saw the expression on Zoë's face. "Too much?"

"Too pukey!" Zoë groaned. "I'd look like Kermit the Frog in that!" Zoë protested.

"Oh, it's not that bad, honey …" Then her mom reconsidered the dress and the corners of her mouth twitched. "Ribbitt!"

That did it. They both dissolved into fits of laughter.

"It really is atrocious, isn't it?" her mother said when they'd gained some semblance of self-control. "What would you suggest?"

Zoë hopped off her bed and rummaged through the closet. "What about this navy dress with the white collar?" She displayed her choice.

"Perfect!" her mom agreed. "I'd best get back downstairs. I left Fatima in the living room perusing an old yearbook from our university days." She started out of the room, then stopped. "And Zoë, for heaven's sake — *no sneakers*."

Zoë changed into the navy dress. Even though she always felt like an old English nanny in it, it beat the green monstrosity, hands down.

She wondered how things had come to this. Was it possible? Could it be? Maybe the reason she hadn't said anything before was because deep down, she actually wanted her mom to figure everything out for her, like she'd done when Zoë was a little girl.

True, the idea of designing cars made her blood tingle and her stomach do twittery things, but that could simply be because, up until recently, she'd felt like a total loser. Wild Child Zoë sure hadn't been known for her wise choices. Maybe before she rejected everything her mom had lined up, she'd do what every school kid knew to do when you were caught in a sudden burst of flame — stop, drop and roll. She'd listen politely at dinner and try to make her mom proud.

Zoë smoothed her hair, ran some gloss over her lips, then rummaged in her closet until she found a pair of dress shoes with honest-to-goodness heels.

***

Dinner was a stroll down memory lane for her mother and Professor Hakeem. Zoë learned more about the good old days than she ever wanted to. Most of it was incredibly boring, but some of the stories about the things her mother had done in her wild youth had Zoë laughing out loud. Who knew her mother was such a daredevil — leading jock-strap raids on the guys' dorm, skinny-dipping in the campus fountain! It was a real eye-opener.

Zoë was sad her father didn't get to hear what a fun girl her mom used to be. He was working late on his campaign, and wouldn't be joining them, as usual.

"… and Zoë, I haven't told you the best part," her mother went on happily chatting.

"What's that, Mother?" Zoë asked, reaching for the ice water.

Her mom and Professor Hakeem exchanged a conspiratorial look. "We were going to save it for an after-dinner surprise, but I guess now is as good a time as any."

"Your mother thought you would enjoy this, Zoë." Professor Hakeem reached into her large purse and took out a thick envelope. "I will, of course, help you all I can when you enter the pre-med program. It's good to know some young people have their future mapped out far in advance, so organized."

She handed Zoë the beige packet with "University of Calgary, Faculty of Medicine" embossed on the outside.

Zoë swallowed. "For me? You shouldn't have. I didn't get you anything …"

"Don't be flip, Zoë, open it." Her mother leaned expectantly toward her daughter and the envelope.

Zoë ripped open the end and took out one of the

sheets. It was an invitation to a private tour of the faculty of medicine, including associated facilities. These included the Foothills Hospital teaching units for all the new prospective doctors, and a special side trip to the Tom Baker Cancer Clinic for the oncologist-wannabes in the crowd. It would be held this Saturday, with a dinner at the Faculty Club to follow in the evening.

"Isn't this for students who are actually going into pre-med?" Zoë asked, holding up the invitation.

"Yes, my dear," Professor Hakeem said. "But when a sister calls for help, we Delta Debs stick together."

Zoë saw the *sorority sister* look pass between them. She thought of Adam's plans for them to watch the Paris–Dakar rally on Saturday. How would she explain this to him? He had no idea her life had been hijacked and was now out of her control.

Her mother should not have done this without consulting her. Talking about university was one thing, but this was something else. She felt like she'd been thrown into some kind of medical school whirlpool, and it was sucking her down.

She wouldn't do it. She needed time to think this through. It was too freaking soon to sign-off on her future! Zoë turned to her mother, the biting words on the tip of her tongue. Then she saw her mom's shining eyes and brilliant smile, and her anger evaporated.

"This is so … so … great, but I haven't even applied for my undergrad yet. Aren't we kind of rushing things?" Zoë finished with a weak smile of her own.

Her mother waved her hand dismissively. "Don't worry about that. Why, you'll be done your undergrad in no time. By living at home with no financial worries you could go to summer school, work right through, and be finished in three years, not four. That would get you on your way a whole year earlier."

Zoë could barely keep up with her pre-planned life.

"I can hardly wait."

Her mom reached out her hand and covered Zoë's. "I'm so proud of you. This is the first step to a successful life." Her eyes momentarily slid to the empty chair where Zoë's father usually sat. "You are making me one happy mom."

Zoë nodded. Any thought of shooting her mom down was now gone. Her stomach fluttered nervously. She knew this was a big moment in her life. After this, there was no going back. She'd be a grown-up Zoë making grown-up decisions. Her dream of being an engineer was only a dream after all. She was in grade twelve, close to graduating, and had done nothing to make it happen. Now, thanks to her mother, she was being fast-tracked to stardom. It was showtime, and Zoë felt sure she was up to the task. She held up her water glass.

"Here's to my new and improved future."

"No more car nonsense?" her mother asked.

Zoë grinned reassuringly at her mom.

"I promise, no more cars, Mom. From now on, it's Zoë Kendall, MD."

Her mother and her new benefactor held up their glasses and joined Zoë in her toast. She looked around the table at the happy faces congratulating her.

In a heartbeat, life had taken an unexpected detour.

***

When Zoë went to bed that night, she felt like she'd taken a firm grip on her future. It was true, she hadn't done anything about securing success for herself, so if her mom wanted to nudge her in a direction she hadn't thought of before, who's to say it wasn't the right thing to do?

In her dream, the sun shone brightly as Zoë watched the sleek car effortlessly take the long left-handed sweeper. It was obvious that it handled beautifully. It floated around the corner with virtually no body roll. Amazing design. Zoë stood at the side of the road, smiling as the perfectly built automobile glided past her. She wanted to see more of the wonderful car, and held up her hand to stop it, but it was already disappearing around the next corner.

Chapter 4

The rest of the week was so peaceful, it made life around the Kendall house pretty sweet. Her mother was practically humming as she busily made plans for their weekend.

Actually, Zoë was getting used to the way things had turned out. She felt like she'd turned a big corner in her life. So what if it wasn't exactly the path she thought she'd be taking? Her mom was ecstatic, and Zoë was sure her dad would be on board when she told him, or as on board as he ever was with life around the house these days, and all she had to do was go along for the ride.

It had taken her a whole lot of soul-searching and rethinking things, but her head was now firmly wrapped around the idea of Zoë Kendall, Cardiac-Thoracic-Jurassic Surgeon. Whatever! It kind of had a nice ring to it.

The idea of being through with cars sucked, but there was through and then there was *through*. Doctors drove kick-ass cars didn't they?

***

Early Friday morning, Zoë was rummaging in the bottom of her backpack for her car keys, when her dad came down the stairs.

"Good morning, princess." He kissed the top of her head. "I was hoping to catch you before you left." He went to his briefcase and took out an envelope. "I've got a little surprise I think you'll enjoy."

Zoë opened the envelope and found three gold-level tickets to the Edmonton Grand Prix in the summer.

"Cool! Oh wow, Dad, this is great!" And it was so like her dad. He believed that when a problem reared its ugly head in the Kendall household, the best solution was to throw cash until it yelled "uncle." It was his way, and besides, she loved going to the Indy. Everyone there was into one thing — racing. She frowned. Three tickets were a little puzzling. She guessed one was for her, one for her dad and, hard as it was to believe, one must be for her mother.

"Does Mom know you bought her a ticket?" Zoë asked quizzically.

Her dad shrugged. "Actually, the third ticket is for Adam. This year, there's going to be a Drifting Competition, lots of tight car control and preci-

sion sliding on pavement. Any girl who handles a rally car like you do will really appreciate the finesse some of those jockeys have with their machines."

Zoë grinned. "I've always wanted to see that, Dad. This is wicked!" She could already imagine it. The "through with cars" thing would have to wait.

"And don't worry about your mother. I'll let her know all about it. I'm sure she'll be pleased."

Zoë was sceptical. "Oh, I'm sure she'll be thrilled." Just then, the other part of what her dad had said registered. "You got Adam a ticket?"

"Well, of course. He's your co-driver isn't he?"

Zoë wasn't sure how to answer. She knew hesitation was deadly with her dad. His lawyer senses would kick in at any second. He'd want to know what was going on, and she'd have to fess up to agreeing to ditch rallying. "Yes, he's co-driving." This was true, but under the new and improved plan, he wouldn't be co-driving with her.

This was something else she had to tell her dad later, much later. Her getting out of rallying would be a serious blow to him, and he had enough on his plate right now. He'd always encouraged her to rally, joking that it was in the Kendall genes. Besides, once she started university, he'd see she was way too busy for cars, and it wouldn't be an issue.

"Speaking of doing things together, are you sure you'll be able to go with us? I kind of noticed you haven't been around a lot lately."

Her dad looked crestfallen. "I know Zoë, but it won't be for long. When things settle down, I plan on having a lot more time free. With work and my campaign, it's a little crunched right now, that's all." He tried to make light of it. "It's a tough job, but someone's got to do it, and princess, there's a lot of people who have faith that I'm the right person for that job."

Zoë could see this was hard for her father. "I know it's important, Daddy. I miss you is all, and I know Mom does too."

He pulled her into a hug. "I miss you too, princess."

Zoë squeezed him back. "I've got to run, Dad. Thanks for the great surprise." She kissed him on the cheek, wondering how it would go when he told her mom about the tickets. She'd make sure she was out of the house when he did.

***

The final bell rang, and Zoë swore the entire high school was making a mad dash for the parking lot all at once. The hallways were a logjam of students flooding toward the exits.

Zoë slammed her locker shut and plunged into the flow of escapees. She'd meet Adam at his car. He'd given her a ride to school that morning, and she hadn't told him a thing about what was going on. Jeez, she was still getting used to it herself.

"Hey, Bunny, wait up!" Adam called as he

waded through the throng to join her. "Can you free up a couple of hours right now?" He slid his arm around her waist.

"You mean after I fight my way out of this mob? Yeah, I guess so. What's shakin'?" She dodged a linebacker-sized girl in coveralls who shoved past her.

"Great. The deal is this. I've been giving the suspension problem some serious thought, and I'm worried that new stuff won't get here in time for the High Mountain Run." He stepped in front of her to shield Zoë from a stampeding herd of cheerleaders rushing down the hall toward the gym. "So, to cover your cute little ass," he gave her butt a quick squeeze and Zoë jumped, "I changed out the springs and shocks, but they may be too stiff, so I need you to take the car for a shakedown spin to make sure it's set up the way you want. We could head out to your folk's place in Kananaskis for a blast. What do you say?"

Zoë didn't know what to say. After her dad's surprise, she'd spent the afternoon trying to convince herself that cars were no longer the most important things in the universe.

Spilling the news about the Indy tickets wouldn't help. There was no way she could dial down her enthusiasm on that one, and it would finish her credibility on the giving-up-cars thing. She could try and explain she was only going to the Indy to make her dad happy, but Adam would see right through her.

Brutal seemed the best way, a clean break. "Gee, Adam, I don't think so. I've got an awful lot of homework to do before I start studying for that mammoth biology exam next week. It's nearly June, and finals will be breathing down our necks in no time."

Zoë knew that if she were going to make her new life plan work, she had to bump up her science marks, especially biology, which wasn't her best subject. She could take a five-speed manual transmission apart and put it back together in her sleep, but dissecting a frog's guts was beyond her.

"*Homework? Biology exam?* Instead of blasting through the woods in our sleek little bullet? Are you kidding me?"

Adam's face looked so funny, Zoë laughed. Maybe a little backsliding wouldn't hurt.

"Fine, but I want it on my permanent record that I think your priorities are bogus." She leaned into Adam and his arm tightened around her protectively. She liked the way they fit together. And besides, this might be their last time working on their car as a team.

"Hey, I have some cool news. My dad got us tickets for the Edmonton Grand Prix in July." Zoë hoped this would take the edge of what was coming.

"No way! That rocks! I heard there'll be drifting there this year." Adam pulled her a little closer.

"It should be a blast." Zoë knew it was going to be nothing but trouble when her mom found out,

but man, she wanted to go so badly. And watching wasn't like driving, right? She'd explain it to her mom somehow. After all, it was only one weekend.

***

The ride out to the Kendall cabin rocked. A rally car had to be street legal, complete with signal lights and mufflers, so despite the full roll cage and them sitting in five-point harnesses wearing intercom helmets, Zoë and Adam were as free to amble through the city streets in the Civic as any other Sunday driver on their way to the country.

True, they got several extremely strange looks and both of them cracked up as onlookers stopped to gawk at the pretty little red rally car. Zoë loved it, then felt a wave of regret as she reminded herself this chapter of her life would soon be closed forever.

Adam chattered all the way out to the Kendall's extremely large log cabin, with its fully equipped garage full of tools and toys that would be the envy of every rallier in the world. Their land bordered the Kananaskis Forest Reserve, and it was here that Zoë's father tested and tweaked all his rally cars, including the Mitsubishi Evo and WRX STi, which she'd hoped to drive herself one day.

Hoped — past tense, past tense, *past* tense, she reminded herself. Now, thanks to her mom, she had a realistic focus for her future, no more putting off growing up.

Well, Zoë grinned as her hand tightened on the wheel, maybe she could focus a whole lot better after one more day of driving. She shifted down and made a sharp left that would take them onto a rutted country road and then a tightly twisting gravel trail, before they blasted up the curving drive to the cabin.

The car took the hairpin corner at the top with very little body roll. Adam had prepped the new shocks and springs exactly right. He really was a genius at twisting wrenches.

Feeling absolutely in sync with the car, she did a perfect handbrake turn, stopping precisely in front of the big garage door. Laughing, they waited for the dust cloud to settle.

"Now, that's what I call a shakedown drive!" Adam grinned. "What did you think, Ms. Kendall?" He held his hand out with an imaginary microphone to capture her comments.

"I'd say you have this thing dialled in exactly, Mr. Harlow."

"That makes me feel a whole lot better, because I got this email from the fabricator." He pulled a piece of paper out of his jacket pocket and handed it to her, then clambered out of the car.

Zoë popped the release on her safety harness and scanned the printout. The new suspension wasn't going to make it in time. "Well, this sucks. He promised he could make the modifications and have it back to us for the rally."Adam helped her climb over the roll cage brace that ran down the

inside of the car to the floor in front of the driver's door.

"I didn't want to upset you, so I thought I'd make sure our little zoom-buggy handled like silk before you saw it." He pulled her against him. "I don't want anything upsetting my favourite driver."

Zoë's arms went around Adam's waist. "Always thinking of team morale." She noticed he hadn't shaved this morning. The look was totally hot.

He leaned down and kissed her awkwardly, their helmets with the cumbersome mic attachment not allowing the kind of contact they both wanted.

"Let me slip into something a little more comfortable. Then you can show me what you did to our car."

Before he could grab her again, she hurried to the garage and unlocked the walk-in door. Adam was in the driver's seat before the big double door was all the way up. Zoë tossed him a set of coveralls as he climbed back out of the car. She'd already zipped up her own pretty pink set, and had two creepers waiting before he'd finished suiting up.

They spent the next two hours going over the modifications and checking the wiring harness for any loose connections that might give them grief. Finally, everything was finished to both their satisfactions.

"Now all we need is more practice time." He

peeled off his coveralls and returned them to their hook on the wall. "What's your schedule like?"

Zoë thought about this weekend, and about how she'd promised her mother *no more cars*. How could she tell Adam any of this? She was feeling so great; she didn't want to spoil their time together. She hung her pink coveralls up and went for her favourite backup — the big stall.

"I'll have to check my Daytimer," she lied. "Come on. Let's get something to drink." Zoë led him to the back door of the cabin. Punching in the code for the keyless entry, they walked into the kitchen. "Let me shut off the security alarm first or we'll have some unwanted company."

Adam followed closely behind her. "And we don't want that."

He kissed the back of her neck as Zoë tried to concentrate on punching the right code into the alarm. "Hey, slow down, hotshot. We're here to work, remember?"

"Yeah, yeah, but all work and no play makes for a dull co-driver." Adam continued to do things to her neck, and now, her ear too.

"I think this kind of play makes for a horny co-driver." Zoë reluctantly pulled out of his embrace. It would be nice to go where Adam wanted, but this could so easily get out of hand, and the guilt she felt at not telling him everything made her romance meter bottom out. "Come on, cowboy, cool your jets." She went to the fridge for pops.

"Hungry?"

"I wouldn't say no to a snack," Adam admitted as he took the cans from her.

"I'll get some pitas and hummus, you take those into the living room." She shooed him out of the kitchen.

They sat on the butter-soft leather sofa and enjoyed their food and drink as they watched the evening closing in through the large panoramic windows. Dust motes danced in the golden light. It was very peaceful, and Zoë felt great. She closed her eyes. The car had performed way better than either of them had expected.

Adam had been playing with her hair as she snuggled up next to him. Now, he traced a design on her thigh with the fingers of his other hand.

Zoë smiled without opening her eyes. "That's the shifting pattern for a six-speed. Are you trying to tell me something?"

"Mmmm," he mumbled as he buried his face in her neck, his lips tracing tiny kisses down to her collarbone.

"Five gears aren't enough for you any more?" she asked, forgetting her previous caution as she moved to kiss him back.

"Depends …" he whispered hoarsely.

"Oh yeah, on what?" she murmured, her tongue now assaulting his ear.

He groaned. "On your power curve."

Her eyes popped open and she sat up. Laughing, she slapped him playfully on the chest.

"You've never complained about any of my curves before!"

"Oh, I'm not complaining." His warm brown eyes told her everything she needed to know.

"What time are you coming over tomorrow to watch the Paris–Dakar rally?" he asked, as they settled back into the couch.

Zoë stiffened, her mood cooling instantly.

"Tomorrow?" It had been the perfect Friday night until now. "Ah, actually, I have a problem with tomorrow night." She couldn't meet his eyes. "I've had a change of plans. Something's come up, a family thing, and I can't make it. I'm sorry, Adam."

She felt like a cheat. Something had come up, all right. She couldn't tell Adam that she'd be at the University of Calgary on the Tour de Jour without telling him also *why* she'd be there, and she wasn't ready to explain all the gory details yet. Adam didn't notice her change of mood. "No worries, Bunny. I know how family can be, and you said your folks were going through a rough patch. It's great you're putting them first."

He kissed her, and the sweetness of his words made her eyes sting. "You're incredible, you know that?" she said, unable to look at him.

"And don't you forget it."

He gave her a little squeeze and Zoë swallowed to stop the sick feeling that welled up in her. Adam was going to freak when she told him she'd changed not just tomorrow's plans, but everything

they'd planned together. For all she knew, he may hate the new Zoë Kendall.

***

Zoë turned restlessly in her sleep. In the failing light of her dream, she watched the big four-door hurtle down the twisting road. She could tell the design was all wrong for what the driver was trying to do. It practically wallowed in the corners. Out of the corner of her eye, she saw a smaller car approaching from the opposite direction. The bulky sedan lost control and slewed sideways, drifting into the path of the oncoming car. Things were about to get ugly. The big tank righted itself and pulled back into its own lane, but for the smaller car, it was too late. The driver couldn't steer the car out of trouble, and had no choice but to hit the ditch to avoid the head-on crash.

Zoë woke with a start, her heart pounding. She turned and peered at the red display on her alarm clock: 4:02 a.m. *Rats!* With a groan, she pulled the pillow over her head. She was going to be a wreck tomorrow.

Chapter 5

Saturday morning arrived early, and with way too much enthusiasm.

Zoë hid under the covers hoping she would be struck with the bubonic plague, or at least one of her blinding migraines, which she hadn't had for over a year now. The migraines knocked her out in a big way, one that would let her off the hook for today.

Her dream-interrupted sleep had been bad enough, but it had been what happened as she'd been getting ready for bed that had really ruined her rest. She'd accidentally overheard a midnight conversation between her mom and dad. Her dad had worked late again, and Zoë's mom had gone ballistic.

Their words had been bitter and Zoë hoped her mom hadn't meant the things she'd said. Later, noises from the kitchen meant her dad couldn't

sleep either and was making himself tea. But it was the sobbing coming from her mother's bedroom that had kept Zoë staring at the ceiling until well past midnight.

Climbing out of her warm, cosy bed, Zoë headed for a hot shower.

Maybe she'd be able to smooth things over at breakfast. In the old days, Saturday morning pumpkin pancakes were always a family favourite. If she hurried, she'd have time to make a stack before her dad came downstairs. She hummed to herself as she turned the hot water on. A little whipped cream wouldn't hurt either.

She was putting the last fragrant pancakes in the oven to keep warm, and had the coffee steaming, when her mom walked into the kitchen.

"Ready for our big day, honey?" she asked, grabbing a tub of yogourt out of the fridge, then going to the cupboard for the granola.

"Where's Dad?" Zoë asked, as her mom set a delicate bone china bowl on the table.

"Your father had to go into the office early. Why?"

Zoë was disappointed but decided to keep trying the pancake ploy with her mom. "I thought I'd make us a big old pile of pumpkin pancakes. There's a stack in the oven waiting for some hungry stranger." Zoë waved her spatula ready to dish up a six-pack.

"Oh, no thanks, honey. I'm trying to watch my carbs."

Her mom dished up the yogourt and added a careful teaspoon of granola. She never saw the frustration on Zoë's face.

"Suit yourself, but I'm pigging out." Zoë took the pancakes out of the oven and put eight fluffy beauties on her plate. After she'd drowned these in maple syrup, she began decorating the cakes with the can of whipped cream — happy face, sad face, confused face, crabby face ... pretty well everything Zoë felt right now.

Her mother frowned. "I can hear your arteries clogging from here. Are you sure you wouldn't rather have a bowl of yogourt? Lots of busy little bugs to keep your gut healthy."

"Wow, Mom, when you put it like that, it's darn hard to resist." She took a giant bite of the whipped-cream slathered, maple-syrup soaked goodness. Her mother continued to watch her.

"Wha ...?" she asked, her mouth too full and dripping syrup.

"I was remembering how your father liked those things." Her mom's voice was a tiny bit wistful, and then an edge came into it. "But apparently, the place will fall down around everyone's ears if he doesn't go into the office every day."

There was a sting in her mom's tone Zoë didn't like. Like it was her dad's fault that he had to work all the time. As if. He was a lawyer; people counted on him. Her mom was being totally unfair!

"Maybe he likes the peace and quiet." The

words were out of Zoë's mouth before she realized what she'd said.

The spoon in her mother's hand stopped halfway to her mouth. "What did you say, young lady?"

Her voice had a razor's edge, and Zoë knew she'd stepped over the line. "I meant he's doubly busy, with work and the by-election coming up. Dad's sure he can get backing for his bid to be nominated. Can you imagine? Dad as member of parliament for our riding?"

Her mother's look told her right away that she'd jumped out of the frying pan and into the fire. After all, it was her dad's plan to fast-track himself to Sussex Drive that had her parents at each other's throats.

"I think you need to mind your own business Zoë, and *leave adult matters to adults*!" Her mother slammed her empty bowl into the dishwasher and left the kitchen.

"Great," Zoë groaned. She had a knack for screwing things up right out of the box, or in this case, before the box was even opened. She threw the rest of the now soggy pancakes into the garbage. They needed a dog.

Of all days to get off on the wrong foot with her mom, this was not the one Zoë would have picked. She knew she should appreciate all her mother had done in arranging this super-tour, but somehow, it was hard to get up for it. Maybe she'd get as excited as her mom once they were actually

trooping around the labs and checking out the cadavers, or whatever gruesome special insider goodies awaited the chosen few.

***

The U of C campus was a rambling green space filled with warm sunshine, tall trees, and a mix of old and new architecture that appealed to Zoë. The small city thrummed with a life of its own. The late May sun had real heat, and she wished she'd worn her ball cap, but that wouldn't have gone with the outfit her mother had suggested. She actually liked the lavender blouse, charcoal pants, and grey checked blazer ensemble. And with the extra makeup, she felt and looked like she belonged, even if it was a bit like playing dress-up. She was more of a jeans and T-shirt kind of girl, but for an occasion like this, she needed to feel confident, and looking the part of a first-class coed helped her do just that. Professor Hakeem, who, Zoë found out, was also a medical doctor and had worked in third world countries with Doctors Without Borders for years, was actually a very funny lady.

Her mother was like a young coed, laughing and joking.

The day was going way better than Zoë had expected after the poor start. They toured the facilities with several other prospective students, all of whom were obviously older and ready to begin their medical studies, but Zoë held her head

up and managed to ask some insightful questions during the Q&A after the tour was finished.

Professor Hakeem, or Fatima, as Zoë now called her, left after the tour, but promised to meet them at the Faculty Club for the dinner.

"I have one more stop," her mother said as she checked her watch. "And I think we should head over right now."

Zoë had no idea where her mother was taking them, but the day was going so well, she decided to stay on this ride till the end. They drove a short distance off campus to a large clapboard house, with pillars flanking the double door on which a brass plaque winked in the bright sunshine.

When they walked up, Zoë saw what was written on the plaque — three Greek letters.

"Delta, Kappa and Phi?"

"Delta, Kappa, Phi!" her mother confirmed, beaming. "This is my old sorority house."

Zoë had no idea sororities still existed in the twenty-first century, but from the music pouring out of the upstairs balcony, the Delta Debs were obviously alive and kickin' it.

A young woman not much older than Zoë greeted them. Her fresh face was devoid of any makeup, and her chinos appeared ironed.

"Hello, and welcome to the Delta Kappa Phi house. Please, won't you come in." She held the door open for Zoë and her mother.

Zoë felt like she was stepping back in time as she followed her mother into the old house.

"I'm guessing you're Melanie." Her mother held out her hand.

"I am, and you must be Mrs. Kendall!" Melanie beamed back. "Professor Hakeem said a sister was stopping by with a prospective pledge," she winked at Zoë, "and I was to give you the ten-cent tour."

Zoë looked over her shoulder to see whom Melanie was referring to as the "prospective pledge," then realized that it was her. Duh!

"Oh, I'm not even accepted to U of C yet," Zoë explained quickly, feeling a little out of her element. Her mother hadn't mentioned anything about joining her old sorority!

"It's never too early to decide on the very best," Melanie laughed as she led them into the living room.

"I couldn't agree more!" Her mother nodded at the immaculate room. "My, you girls certainly keep it tidier than when I lived here!"

Melanie blushed. "Actually, this is probably not an accurate representation of life at Delta House. I sort of brought out the firehose when I heard we were having company."

"Whew! You had me worried for a minute!" Zoë's mother laughed. "I don't think Zoë would fit in here at this neatness level."

Zoë frowned at her mom. She wasn't exactly a slob at home … okay, maybe verging on piggy. But she'd always thought too much cleanliness was unhealthy: no challenge for a girl's immune

system if there were no germs lurking under her bed in old peanut butter jars or empty chip bags.

Melanie put her arm around Zoë. "In that case, come on, I'll show you what this joint is really like!"

They toured the rest of the house, complete with piles of laundry, dirty dishes, and overflowing trash bins. Zoë had to admit she felt right at home.

She was examining some old framed photos in a hallway, when one of them made her stop in her tracks. There was a faded picture of her mother and some of her sorority sisters smiling at her. Zoë gulped. The outfit her mom had been wearing was almost identical to the one she'd picked out for Zoë this morning! Yuck! Zoë decided that would be the last time her mom helped her pick out "exactly the right ensemble for the occasion, dear."

Stories were told over cold pops, and Zoë thought seeing this side of her mother was cool. Somehow, she felt closer, now that she was getting a glimpse of her mom's misspent youth. It made Zoë feel like she understood her mother better.

At one point, Melanie put on a CD and the topic of dancing came up.

"I love to dance," Melanie giggled. "It's the only aerobic exercise I seem to get."

"I used to be pretty good at shakin' it myself," Zoë's mom laughed.

"You're kidding, right, Mom?" Zoë was having

trouble imagining her mom doing the Macarena or vogue, or whatever Neolithic war dance they would have done that long ago.

"Oh Zoë, you should have seen me! I was something." And with that, her mom jumped up and pulled Zoë to her feet. She broke into a bizarre dance, gyrating enthusiastically and with no apparent rules.

Zoë stood frozen, then decided to show her mom what real dancing was all about. She busted a move any rapper would have been proud of.

This proved too much for their hostess, and Melanie joined in. All three ended up slumped on the couch in fits of hysterical laughter.

Zoë couldn't believe her mother! She was a blast.

"Oh, it wasn't all fun and games." Her mom laughed, fanning herself and taking a sip of a fresh drink. "Academic standards were strictly enforced. You could always count on several Delta Debs being on the dean's list in any given semester. I was a regular myself." Her eyes had a faraway look in them.

As the time for the scheduled dinner at the Faculty Club approached, Zoë and her mother thanked the young coed for all the warm Delta House hospitality.

"And I think I can safely say we'll all be thrilled when you're pledged here next fall." Melanie hugged Zoë as she left.

"Great!" Zoë said, not knowing how else to respond.

When they climbed into the car, her mother reached behind the seat and brought out a beautifully wrapped box. "This is for you." She waited expectantly while Zoë opened the ribbon-festooned present.

Inside was a pink-and-white jacket with the Delta Kappa Phi symbols embroidered on the front.

Her mom lovingly ran her fingers over the Greek symbols. "It was mine, and I thought you might like it." She smiled, and Zoë thought she seemed almost shy when she added: "Maybe we'll start a new family tradition. You know, all the Kendall women are Delta Kappa Phi. One day, who knows, maybe your daughter will be a Delta Deb."

"Gee, Mom, I don't know what to say." It was true. Zoë was speechless. University, mentors, and now a sorority! She put the lid back on the box before any more of her mother's surprises could spring out.

Things were moving way too fast, and not being the one behind the wheel made Zoë nervous and, if she were being honest, a little ticked off. It seemed her mom had thought of everything to make sure Zoë didn't wander off the carefully planned course she'd mapped out for her.

Chapter 6

Zoë's eyes flew open as she sat bolt upright in her bed. She was covered in sweat and her head was throbbing. This nightmare was worse than anything she'd had before.

It had started like her others. She'd been standing at the side of a road, when a car had approached from down the shadowy highway. At that moment, Zoë saw another vehicle speeding from the opposite direction. It was going to be a head-on collision! She dropped the box she'd been holding and frantically waved her hands at the oncoming car, trying in vain to alert the driver. This time, the cars had not missed each other. When they hit, both cars disintegrated into shards of splintered plastic and glass. Flames roared out of what was left of the passenger compartment of the shiny new car, where helpless crash victims clawed at the windows. Inside the box at her feet

were the new safety designs she'd been working on. Zoë knew those designs were meant for the burning car.

The dream had been so real. She could still feel the heat from the flames. If designing cars meant she'd have nightmares like this, she was glad she'd switched career paths! No way did she want another screamer like that one.

Zoë shook off the gruesome nightmare and tried to psych herself up to start her day. She'd stayed up late studying for today's mega biology exam. By the time she'd finally hit the hay, she'd felt she had a good grasp on everything they'd covered in class. She was ready to face whatever their teacher would throw at them, and in the dissection lab, that covered a load of truly gross stuff.

Something familiar about the pounding in her temples made Zoë pray this headache wouldn't turn into a migraine. It had been over a year since she'd had one of the head-exploding episodes, and she didn't have any of her special medicine on hand. It was administered with a needle, which Zoë hated, but she hated the headaches more.

Her mother was waiting at the breakfast table when she came downstairs.

"Good morning, honey. I made scrambled eggs." Wearing what could only be called a tailored jogging suit, her mom poured coffee into a mug and set it down in front of Zoë. "I've also been giving some thought to the fall and university."

Zoë wondered if the little man in her skull with

the sledgehammer would knock off for breakfast. Her stomach was queasy and the smell of the eggs was nauseating. She rubbed her temples. "I can't think about that now, Mother."

"I simply wanted to tell you …"

"I said I don't want to talk about it!" Zoë snapped. Her mother stared at her in surprise, and Zoë instantly felt like something you scrape off the bottom of your sneaker. "Sorry, Mom. I … I have this big test, and I'm a little freaked out about it, that's all." She squinted, wishing the venetian blinds were closed on the wide bay window.

Her mother blinked as though resetting her switches. "It's okay, honey. I understand. Still, you should have a good breakfast if you're going to write an exam. Food for the brain."

The fumes from the eggs assaulted Zoë's nose again. "I've got to get to school early so I can go over my notes." The bright sunlight streaming through the window stabbed her eyes. "I'll catch you later."

"But Zoë, it's only seven o'clock in the morning!"

"Got to go, Mom." Zoë grabbed her backpack and headed outside into fresh air, away from the smell of those eggs!

Fumbling in her pocket, she found the keys, opened the car door, and fell behind the wheel. Frantically, she searched for her sunglasses and slid them on.

The familiar sparkling aura hit halfway to

school and Zoë pulled over to the side of the road and waited.

"Oh man, not now!" she moaned, knowing the strange lights in her peripheral vision meant her headache was about to move to a whole other level.

A couple of moments later, everything went black, and all she could hear was a loud buzzing in her ears. This was going to be a full-blown head-exploder, and from painful experience, she knew that in twenty minutes she was going to be completely wrecked.

The injectable medication worked great, but she hadn't needed any for so long, the prescription had expired. There was no way she could get more without a new note from her doctor.

After several minutes the vision and hearing loss passed, and Zoë rummaged in her backpack for her cell phone. Kayla Strong was a good friend who also got migraines, though not as severe as Zoë's. She'd have meds, and wasn't that what good friends were for — to help out in a dire emergency? Kayla was Zoë's only shot at being able to write the exam. She misdialed twice, but finally got through.

"Hey Kayla, it's me," Zoë croaked. "Can you bring me some of your migraine juju? I'm getting a nasty one, and I need to head it off at the pass."

"Zoë, you sound like crap and you are so in luck. I restocked a couple of days ago, but it's not the same stuff you take, no spike."

Kayla's voice was very loud and Zoë pulled the phone away from her ear. "No worries. Bring what you have. I'll be the one moaning in the can when you get to school."

Zoë flipped her phone shut and rubbed her forehead, pressing so hard she left red welts on her skin. Although it was a different drug, Zoë hoped Kayla's meds would work. Arriving at school with her stomach rumbling ominously, Zoë went directly to the washroom. In a matter of minutes, she'd be throwing up and wishing she were dead.

An hour later, she was resting her head against the cool porcelain of the toilet when she heard her name.

"Zoë, you in here?" Kayla whispered, incredibly loudly.

"Back here …" Zoë struggled to her feet and stumbled out of the stall to the sink where she sloshed her sour mouth with water.

"Whoa, girlfriend, you auditioning for lead in *The Zombie from Planet X*? Maybe you should go home." Kayla handed her the tablets. She was dressed in a retro army-fatigue combo with a T-shirt proclaiming *Reading Rocks!* Her dyed red hair was gelled outrageously and complemented the eyebrow piercing.

"I will after Duncan's stinking bio exam." Zoë tossed the pills down, then ran water over a paper towel. Holding the soggy towel to her forehead, she smiled weakly at her friend. "You saved my life. Thanks."

Kayla shook her head. "No problem, but I still think you should bail on Mr. D. God knows he loves tests. This is the sixth test, and only the highest four count for crying out loud. The man's exam crazy. He's sure to dump another little gem on us before the end of June."

"I'll be okay. I need a high bio mark, and besides, I spent last night studying and I wouldn't want to waste all that effort." Zoë winced as the bell shrieked, announcing first period, which, as the Great Exam God's idea of a huge joke, was her biology class.

The medication didn't work nearly as well as her injections, but somehow Zoë managed to finish the written section. She'd struggled with a lot of the questions, her mind refusing to remember what she was sure she knew, then it was on to the lab for the organ dissection.

At her station, she pulled the cover off her specimen and almost threw up again. A large cow's eye stared balefully up at her, as though it knew she didn't want to be here. Anatomy was not Zoë's strong point and dissecting an eyeball was about the worst of worst-case scenarios.

She arranged her tray according to lab protocol, then picked up her scalpel. "I've got a really bad feeling about this," she whispered, as she prepared to do battle with the bovine eyeball.

When she applied pressure to the outer membrane, the orb shuddered, then, as though trying to make a desperate break for freedom, it shot out of her specimen dish and flew across the lab! The eye bounced twice on the cold tile floor and came to rest under Mr. Duncan's desk.

Zoë stared in stunned shock. Of all the rotten things she'd predicted might happen today, this had not been on her list.

Her teacher glared at her over the top of his narrow reading glasses. His cavernous nostrils flared like two black tunnels. A short man, who tended toward chubbiness, he reminded Zoë of Jabba the Hutt. From the way he licked his thick lips, she wondered if he were going to snake out a reptilian tongue and slurp up the runaway sphere.

Wincing, Zoë got up from her station and walked slowly to the front of the room. Mr. Duncan's cold eyes followed her like a spider watching a helpless fly as she knelt on the floor in front of his desk and, reaching under, searched for the wandering eyeball.

Her fingers closed around the squishy specimen. Standing, Zoë opened her hand. The milky orb, now oozing a foul gooey liquid, was coated in dust bunnies and looked like something out of a B movie — *The Curse of the Hairy Eyeball!*

With an apologetic shrug to her scowling teacher, Zoë returned to her desk. She proceeded to chop up the slightly used, and now dented, organ as best she could while her out-of-focus medicated brain dredged up the complicated list of names associated with all the various parts. She'd known them cold last night, but now it was like trying to remember a foreign language!

When the bell rang signalling the end of the exam, Zoë knew she'd bombed the test. Life sucked ... big time!

She trudged to her locker and deposited her textbooks. She couldn't face another class. The medication was wearing off, and she could feel her headache ramping up again. She'd stop at the drugstore and beg the pharmacist to phone her doctor for the real deal. She was desperate.

On the way to the parking lot, Zoë thought of Adam. Poor guy. He probably thought she was avoiding him, which she was, but that was beside the point. At least now, she had a legitimate excuse — her skull was screwed on too tight and the bolts were jamming into her brain.

She spotted his car in the parking lot, and decided to leave a note explaining that she had a horrible headache, and that she'd gone home early. They could touch base tomorrow.

She was tucking the note under his wiper when a hand on her arm caused her to spin around. Dizziness engulfed her as she clutched her head to keep it from flying off her shoulders.

"Hey, I've been trying to get hold of you. I wondered why you didn't call to find out about the Paris–Dakar. Man, that rally is brutal ..." Adam stopped talking when he saw her face. "Jeez, Bunny, you look awful."

"You really know how to make a girl feel special, Adam." Zoë frowned — even the effort of talking was painful. "Sunday, I had to study for my bio exam, and now I have a migraine that's going to put me out of action for at least a day."

"Migraine? I didn't know you got those. I heard they can be wicked."

His voice sounded sympathetic, but although Zoë wanted to be nice, she had to fight the urge get into her car, and simply go home and hide under a blanket.

"I have to go. I'll talk to you later."

"Maybe you shouldn't drive. Do you want me to take you home?"

For some reason, this ticked Zoë off. She was quite capable of herding her little car home, even with her skull pounding. She shook her head a fraction of a millimetre, sending lightning bolts ricocheting around her brain. "No, I'll be okay," she mumbled as she walked to her car.

Adam stayed by her side. "I can come over later with your homework assignments."

"No," was all she had the strength to say.

"I don't mind. I'll worry about you anyway."

He was so sweet Zoë could feel her blood sugar level rising along with her temper. She stopped and glanced up at him, knowing her eyes looked like she was bleeding to death from the inside and her breath was garbage-can gross, another added bonus from her headaches. Having Adam come to her house wasn't what she wanted at all — especially when her chatterbox mother was sure to blab about Zoë's wonderful future and all the wonderful plans she had to become a wonderful freakin' doctor.

She'd break the news in a more private place, like the dark side of the moon maybe. Zoë squeezed her eyes together and gave it one last shot. She was at the end of her rope, both physically and emotionally.

"Adam, I said no." she snapped. "I'll call you."

She climbed into her car and left without looking back.

Chapter 7

Kayla stopped by that evening sticking her head into the darkened cave also known as Zoë's bedroom.

"Dude, I won't stay," she whispered. "I wanted to make sure you made it to your crib okay. Talk to you when you come up for air."

Kayla was about to close the bedroom door when Zoë dragged away the T-shirt she'd been using to shield her eyes.

"No, don't go," she croaked. "I'm feeling tons better. Honest." Being careful not to jar herself, Zoë gingerly sat up and turned on the bedside lamp, blinking rapidly as the bright light assaulted her.

"Yeah, I can tell you're ready to go clubbing." Kayla snorted. "We both know these things squeeze the life out of you for days." She smiled, and the tiny ruby embedded in her front tooth winked in the light.

Tonight she was dressed all in black, and Zoë knew Kayla had worn the soothing colour on purpose. It was much appreciated. Usually Kayla wore so many sequins and sparkling things on her outfits, satellites could see her from orbit.

"I'm not arguing the screamers suck," Zoë said, "but I do feel better. The vet gave me some of my high-test drugs and I'm over the worst. Care for a cocktail?" She offered her friend a glass of the orange juice her mom had left.

"Sure, but only one, I'm driving."

They sipped on their juice as Kayla brought Zoë up to speed on homework, gossip, and anything she'd missed in the day she'd been away. Zoë tried to look interested, but knew she wasn't being convincing.

When the conversation lagged, Kayla pinned Zoë with a laser stare. "Okay, girlfriend, what's buggin' you? You are *so* bummed, and I know it's not from the headache."

Zoë hadn't realized she'd been so transparent, but she couldn't seem to stop worrying about the mess she called her life. She'd tried ignoring everything, but some things wouldn't go away. Telling Kayla the whole sorry story didn't seem right. Why dump it on her friend?

"Stuff. Nothing you want to hear about," she answered evasively.

"No, *stuff* is what grows at the bottom of the fridge when you leave old lettuce alone for a month. I want to know what's got you twisted."

She leaned forward. "And I'm not leaving till you spill it. Friends don't let friends sulk alone."

Zoë nodded tiredly. "Okay, but don't say I didn't warn you. It's like this …" She explained about her mom and dad having problems, and her fears of them splitting.

"Hey, I've been down that nasty little path with my own parents and I wouldn't wish it on anyone," Kayla said sympathetically.

"And good old Trent is spiralling toward the Big Drain of Life."

Again, Kayla understood. "A wise philosopher once said, 'You can pick your friends and you can pick your nose, but you can't pick your relatives'."

Trying to stay calm, Zoë went on. "And then there's my mom's master plan for the rest of my life. She wants me to go to medical school here at U of C and become Banting or Best, I'm not sure which."

Kayla's pencilled brows knitted together. "But I thought you and Adam were going east and getting your engineering degrees?"

"We'd talked about it, but I never did anything to make that happen. I don't know, maybe I was doing the old tried-and-true Zoë tactic, leaving it so late, the choice was taken out of my hands. My mom stepped up so I thought it was a kind of sign that this whole med school thing was meant to be. I'm not kidding, everything is going super smoothly."

"What does Adam think of all this."

Zoë studiously rubbed a drop of juice off the edge of her patchwork comforter.

"You haven't told him!"

Kayla practically yelled and Zoë winced. "No, I haven't told him. I don't know how."

"You're right. You are doing the Zoë Kendall leave-it-till-it-dies-a-natural-death thing, but with Adam. Come on, girlfriend, that stinks. The guy has a right to know. That is, if you intend to go ahead with the new game plan."

"I keep jumping back and forth. It would really make my mom happy, and she deserves to see one of her kids do well. Trent's about to get turfed from McGill. Then there's my dad — if his plan works, he could end up being the head cheese in Ottawa, and I know a doctor daughter would make points with the media."

"Zoë, you're missing the big picture. What is your true bliss?" Kayla pointed at her with a finger sporting a red dragon decal on its black nail. "If you ever want to advance to a higher plane, you have to find out what it is and follow it."

Zoë's head was pounding again. "I guess I want to be Dr. Kendall. It's the best thing." Kayla gave her an *Oh really* smirk as Zoë rubbed her temples. "Honest, Kayla, I want to be a doctor and I'll kick ass doing it!"

Kayla said nothing as she took a sip of her warm orange juice.

Zoë smiled weakly at her friend, but the effort made the throbbing in her skull turn into a drum solo.

Chapter 8

By Wednesday, Zoë was starting to feel human, and was ready to face classes again. She wasn't looking forward to discovering how low her biology mark had sunk.

Stopping by the study on her way out, Zoë unplugged her cell phone from its charger. It had stopped working and she hoped it was something as simple as a dead battery. She pressed the on switch, but nothing happened. Great! And life hands Zoë Kendall another annoying surprise! She couldn't function without her cell, which meant she had to try and fix the problem. Pulling a small screwdriver out of her pack, she set to work. She always had a few tools on her in case of a mechanical failure with one of the million electronic gizmos she carried — cell phone, iPod, appointment calendar, dictionary, calculator, the list went on. Pulling apart the tiny phone, she checked for loose connections.

"What on earth are you doing Zoë?" her mother asked as she entered the study.

"My dumb phone is dead and that won't cut it. Aha!" she crowed, peering inside the small device. "I see the problem. One of the leads is detached and that means soldering it back on, which is a job for later, when I have more time." She put the phone back together and dropped it and the screwdriver into her pack. "I guess I'll be incommunicado today."

Her mother shook her head. "You've always had a way with mechanical things, Zoë. Maybe you could check my blow-dryer later?"

"Actually, Mom, I'm better with electrical wiring harnesses in cars, but a short is a short. Leave it out and I'll take a peek at it later."

Her mother frowned, then changed the subject. "Speaking of things not working right, how's the head?"

"Practically perfect." Zoë tapped her skull. "The voodoo works as well as ever."

"What I don't understand, dear, is why you got one of those nasty things in the first place. Previously, they were stress, induced, but your new plans are going so well.

Zoë thought about everything going on in her life. Nope, no stress here! "I may have one or two things still on my plate, Mom."

"Well, if there's anything I can do to help, let me know." Her mother hugged her. "Zoë, you can always come to me if something is bothering you. You know I'm your biggest cheerleader."

Zoë rolled her eyes. "Gotcha. No worries, Mom. Everything is on track! I'd better jet." She kissed her mother on the cheek. "Have a great day."

She looked for her hoodie, remembered it was in her room, and sprinted upstairs. Adam was picking her up this morning and it wasn't going to be fun.

When he'd called, Zoë knew she couldn't stall any longer. Kayla was right. Telling Adam everything that was going on was a must, but the idea sucked. Hearts were going to be broken, no doubt about that.

In her room, the box with the sorority jacket caught her eye. It was sitting on the chair by the window, where Zoë had put it after their excursion to the university. In the early morning light, the white box appeared to be made out of mother-of-pearl.

Zoë walked over and lifted the lid. The pretty jacket winked at her from the nest of pristine white tissue paper. She ran her fingers over the delicate symbols. It really was beautiful. The idea of being a Delta Deb was kind of growing on her.

Zoë lifted the coat out and tried it on. Glancing into the mirror, she examined the oddly dressed girl looking back. Zoë Kendall in a sorority jacket was too weird, but she had to admit, she looked kind of ... well, to be honest, she looked hot!

Smiling, Zoë took the jacket off and gently replaced it in the box.

Through her window, she spotted Adam pulling into the driveway in his '92 beater Honda. It was obvious all Adam's energy went straight into the pretty red rally car. Grabbing her hoodie, she went out to face the inevitable.

Sliding into the passenger's seat, Zoë prepared for the fireworks.

"How are you feeling, Bunny?" Adam asked as he pulled smoothly into traffic.

"Fine, the proper drugs can do wonders." Zoë cleared her throat. "Adam, about the last few days …"

His brown eyes were warm and smiling. "Hey, you've had a lot going on." He patted her thigh. "I must admit, it was odd when you never asked me about the rally."

A twinge of guilt pinched Zoë for a moment. "Adam, about our rallying. Actually, I've been rethinking things a little, you know, reassessing my time and everything. With university entrance exams coming up, I've got to work on my marks. That bio exam I wrote was a disaster. I'm talking total failure." She thought of her dismal effort in the lab. It really bugged her that she'd bombed when she knew that stuff, but it had been impossible to concentrate with those hammers pounding holes in her skull. "So maybe I won't be able to spend as much time working on cars or watching rallies for a while."

Adam was silent, giving her words serious thought. "You know, you're probably right. When I left for Saudi Arabia last year, I was an A student, but all the travelling really did a number on my grades. You know I've had to repeat several courses so my marks would be high enough to get into engineering. I can understand sacrifices have to be made. What I'm trying to say is, I guess I should cut you some slack."

Zoë thought she heard something strange in his voice, but dismissed it. This was turning out easier than she thought. "I'm glad you understand. We both need to focus on our futures … *individually*."

Adam wheeled the car into the parking lot at school. "Absolutely, and I'm willing to give you some space …" He shut off the ignition and faced her. "But first you have to tell me what the hell is going on."

Zoë was taken aback. In a heartbeat Adam's tone had changed completely, and she didn't like the change at all. His eyes had gone from warm and smiling to cool and calculating.

"I've known you for years, Zoë, and I care about you, so when I see you going off the rails, I want to find out why. I went along with the parent problem thing, being busy with the family stuff, and I know getting sick wasn't your fault. But usually when someone is sick, they let friends know when they get better. It ticked me off when you didn't call. If I hadn't cornered you this morning, I doubt you would have talked to me today either."

He ran his hand through his short brown hair. "We've always been able to talk, and up until now, we haven't had any secrets. So out with it — what are you hiding?"

Zoë didn't like his third degree, even if she deserved it. She also didn't like being put on the defensive, and everyone knows a cornered rat is a dangerous rodent.

"I don't know what you're talking about."

"Don't hand me that crap!" he snapped. "You've been avoiding me; you're evasive when we talk. For crying out loud, I haven't seen you for days, and you didn't even kiss me hello when I picked you up this morning!"

"Is that what this inquisition is about?" Zoë was desperate now and her logic circuits weren't working properly. She gave him a cheap shot, knowing it was unfair. "You're worried because I might not put out for you? Well, let me tell you something, Adam Harlow, I won't let you or any other jock push me into having sex!" She emphasized the point by jabbing her finger at his chest.

She might as well have hit him with a two-by-four.

"What the hell are you talking about? You make me sound like some kind of pervert!"

"You know exactly what I mean. Sex is not something that should be used as a weapon — for good or evil!" Zoë thought she sounded completely righteous, if maybe a bit wacked.

Adam's voice was low and controlled. "Have you gone *totally* nuts?" he exclaimed. "This has nothing to do with sex! And, the last time I checked, using sex as a weapon has never been an issue with us."

"And it's not going to be one now!" Zoë grabbed her pack and reached for the door handle.

"Oh, no you don't!" Adam leaned across her and hit the lock button. "We're not even close to being done."

Zoë knew that tone. When he wanted, Adam could be a bit of a bulldog. She sat back with a sigh. There was no getting away.

"Okay, it's like this. We'd tossed around the idea of the two of us taking engineering together ..."

"What do you mean *tossed around the idea*? We've made definite plans, you and I are going to apply to the University of Ontario, end of story."

Zoë hesitated. "I've changed my mind. I'm going to the University of Calgary."

"What about the Automotive Centre of Excellence?"

She twisted the strap on her backpack, avoiding his gaze. "I've rethought that too. Adam, I'm going to study medicine and go through to be a doctor." There, she'd said it.

"A what?" He stared at her bewildered.

"A doctor. I know this is sudden, but I've been giving it a lot of thought and my mom is in total agreement. Being a physician is a dream anyone would want." She held her chin up defiantly.

"Yes, it's a great career, but not for you, Zoë. The last time I got a bloody nose, you practically passed out. You've wanted to design cars forever." He took her hand in his. "Even if you don't want to go down east, U of C has a first rate engineering department. You could get your degree here."

Zoë felt she was committed now. "I've made up my mind. I'm going into medicine."

"Don't you think it would have been nice if you'd told me you'd blown our plans out of the water? What about us, Zoë? Does this new brighter future have any room for you and me?"

He waited and Zoë swallowed. "Long distance romances sometimes work." They both knew this was rarely the case, and they were facing four long years, not counting post-grad. "You could change your plans and go to U of C too," she offered helpfully.

"So it would be okay for me to turn my life upside down because you've had some sort of epiphany and think you want to be a doctor, but you didn't even have the courtesy to tell me any of this?" His face grew dark.

She felt her temper flare again. "I don't *think* I want to be a doctor, I *know* I want to, and you should respect my decision. I've outgrown cars and rallying. I want to do something more important with my life."

"I do respect your decision, Zoë, but it's hard for me to believe, that's all. You've never said a word about this before, and as for outgrowing cars, I didn't realize it was something you needed to *outgrow*, like braces."

His eyes searched hers and she turned away. Zoë tried to control the unreasonable anger she felt. She knew Adam was not wrong on this one, but why couldn't he simply accept her new choice? People did change their minds on things.

When she took a quick peek at his downcast face, her heart melted. She was afraid she was going to do something stupid, like cry.

"We better get inside. The bell is going to ring." She released the door lock.

Adam slowly climbed out of the car. He never said a word as they walked into school. He didn't try to hold her hand either.

***

Biology class was everything she hoped it wouldn't be and more. When she got her exam back, she stared at the failing mark written at the top of the page — and the failing mark stared right back.

She'd bombed so spectacularly, Mr. Duncan had added a note telling her he wanted to see her after last bell. Great! Things kept getting better and better.

As the morning wore on, Zoë felt the universe was conspiring to tick her off, and it was succeeding in a big way. She opened her locker and every book, binder, empty juice box, and leftover lunch bag fell on top of her; the seam split on her shoe, so that her toes stuck out on one foot; and when she made her way through the aggravating noisy horde in the cafeteria, there was no meatless lasagna left!

Behind the lunch counter, Mrs. Patel was having trouble understanding what Zoë meant when she asked if there was any more of the veggie variety tucked away.

"I'm a *veg-e-tar-i-an*!" She pronounced each syllable in the word, hoping the meaning would become clearer. "That means I don't eat dead animal flesh. I want more of the vegetarian one." Zoë pointed to the empty tray. Her patience was disappearing and the language barrier she and the lunch-counter lady were having was going to get one of them killed. "No meat! *No Meat!*"

"Oh yes, yes indeed, we have meat!" Mrs. Patel nodded enthusiastically, pointing proudly at the tray of regular lasagna.

"No, no, I'm obviously not making myself clear …" Zoë pointed also. "You see that grey mystery sludge oozing out from between those layers of white noodles? *I don't eat that!*" She wondered if screaming would help. Instead, she sighed and admitted defeat.

"I'm sorry, Mrs. P. Lunch hour is too short to do this. I'll have a bottled water and a bun please."

Bread and water suited her mood better anyway.

"I saved the last piece of veggie for you."

She turned to see Adam holding out his tray. In

79

the middle was a plate with the slice of vegetarian lasagna, accompanied by a happy green salad.

Zoë took the tray. "Ah, thanks."

His mouth crooked into a ghost of a smile. "I've got to get going. I'm late for basketball practice." And with that, he turned and walked away.

Was this his way of making up? Zoë wanted to run after him, to try and explain everything again, only better this time. Instead, she watched him leave, knowing he was not the bad guy here.

By the time last class ended, the anger that had kept Zoë fired up all day was gone and left her exhausted. When the bell rang, she was ready to leave and never come back. Grabbing her books, all she wanted was to go home and sleep — then she remembered Adam had given her a ride to school. Great. There was no way she wanted to face him again. Which meant she had only one option — to walk home.

She strode down the hallway, the blown-out toe of her shoe making slapping noises on the polished tiles. Outside, the sky was threatening rain.

Zoë started across the parking lot as the first fat drops hit the hot pavement.

Chapter 9

The minute Zoë walked in the door, she knew something was up.

Her mother was waiting and her face told Zoë there was trouble on the island, and she was the one getting voted off.

"Hi, what's shakin'?" she asked, then in a feeble attempt at humour, held up her backpack and jiggled the worst of the water off before dropping it next to the hall table. She and her backpack were both soaked, thanks to the steady rain that had followed her home.

"Zoë! For heaven's sake, wipe that mess up immediately!" Her mother indicated the closet where a mop was stored for such drippy emergencies. "How was school?"

Her mother's voice had that edge to it that made you want to run to the nearest bomb shelter.

"Ah, fine. Why?' Zoë asked apprehensively as

she swiped at the water with the mop.

"I got a call from Mr. Duncan."

The meeting after school! Zoë had completely spaced it.

"Oh man! I was supposed to stop by Mr. D's room to talk about …" She winced.

"To talk about how you failed a very important biology exam." Her mother shook her head. "Zoë, what happened? Your marks have always been so good. And biology, of all the subjects to do poorly in."

Zoë could see her mother was really upset. "Okay, I had a problem with the exam. But Mom, I knew that stuff, I really did. That was the day I had my migraine, and Kayla gave me some of her meds, but they didn't work very well. I thought I could write it anyway, and I guess, I guess …" Her shoulders slumped. "I guess I messed up."

Her mother gave Zoë's arm a sympathetic squeeze. "I told Mr. Duncan you'd be in his office tomorrow morning, before class. What I don't understand is, if you had a migraine, why didn't you ask to write the exam on another day?"

Zoë had to admit she didn't know why she hadn't ditched the exam. Her doctor would have given her a note. "Because I'm an idiot and I wasn't thinking straight."

The phone shrilled and her mom frowned. "We don't need to tell your father about this. And please, don't forget to visit Mr. Duncan tomorrow morning."

She left to get the phone and Zoë trudged up stairs. How had she forgotten the meeting with Duncan? And as for telling her father, she'd hardly seen him all week, so there was no chance the first thing out of her mouth would be that she'd failed an exam.

Zoë changed her clothes and dried her hair, then went to help her mom with supper.

Her mother was sitting at the kitchen table with a coffee when Zoë walked in. She looked strained and Zoë wondered, what now?

"That was your brother on the phone. He's been suspended from school."

"Oh, man!" With everything else going on, why did her brother have to pick now to pull a Trent. "What's going to happen?"

"Your father will catch the red-eye and fly down to see if he can't straighten everything out, or at least get to the bottom of what happened. Trent was pretty vague about the details."

Now there was a surprise, Zoë thought, Trent being vague about screwing up. And of course, when poor Trent had a problem, her parents moved heaven and earth to fix it. Her dad was going to ride in to her brother's rescue — again!

And what did Zoë get when she had a tiny problem with one stinking exam and one silly meeting? Lined up against the wall with the firing squad all too eager to take aim!

Striding to the cupboard, she grabbed a mug. This was beyond belief! She poured a slosh of coffee into the cup, then banged the pot back down. "So Dad is going make all Trent's problems go away again? Don't you think it's time to let him clean up his own messes? For crying out loud, Trent's supposed to be an adult!" She yanked open the refrigerator door, then, spying the coffee creamer on the counter, shut it again with a little more force than she'd meant.

"That's enough slamming around young lady! Trent has a medical condition, and your father needs to help with the fallout. You should be glad you're so healthy and don't have the challenges your brother does." Her mother set her own cup down so hard that some of the contents slopped over the side.

"Damn! Now look what you made me do!"

"Me!" Zoë exclaimed. "Put the blame where it belongs — you're upset because Trent let you down *again*. Don't try hanging this on me."

They stared at each other, neither willing to back down.

Finally, Zoë relented. "I'm sorry, Mom. Forget I said that junk. I guess that messing up thing is sticking." She sat next to her mother and tried to think of something comforting to say. Her own life might be hell, but her mom's was no picnic either.

"You're right. I remember what a space case Trent can be. He was a pain to live with. I can't imagine what it must have been like for you, or for Trent, always being out of control, never feeling like he owned himself. It would have been tough."

She touched her cup to the rim of her mom's. "Here's to Dad! He's a problem-solver and I'm sure things will get ironed out."

She grinned impishly. "Dr. Zoë prescribes a large dose of Chinese herbs to cure what ails us. How about Imperial Dragon takeout? Best food around, and it always makes me feel better."

Her mom smiled at Zoë's attempt to lighten things. "You know, it makes me feel better too. Where's the phone book, Doc?"

***

That night Zoë had another terrifying dream, this one worse than all the rest. It was pitch dark with pouring rain. Flashes of lightning illuminated a shadowy road on which rally cars flipped and rolled, gas tanks exploded, and mutilated bodies burned. All the usual mayhem delivered in bad action flicks. Through the chaos, Zoë stood by uselessly and watched. By the time her alarm clock went off, she felt like she needed a week in intensive care.

Zoë left home early and was waiting outside Mr. Duncan's room when he arrived.

"Come in, Zoë." He opened the door and ushered her in. "I'm not used to students cancelling appointments with me. What happened to you yesterday?"

Zoë felt cornered. "I know this sounds bad, but I sort of ... forgot."

"You *forgot*!' His face went bright red. "If ditching the meeting was your idea of showing me who was boss, you made a serious misjudgment."

"Honest, Mr. Duncan, I didn't do it to tick you off. I really did forget."

"In light of your exam mark, I find it hard to believe you'd take this so casually. Neither your mother nor I expected this from you at this critical stage of your academic career. If this is any indication of the way things are going, I'd say you're heading down the wrong path. Zoë, I would expect problem behaviour from your brother, but I am really surprised at you."

Zoë cringed. Thanks again for setting the bar so low, Trent!

And why was everyone so concerned with what she did with her life? She sat quietly and listened while her teacher continued his sermon. She nodded occasionally, hoping she passed as a concerned, contrite, sincere student. Finally, the bell rang.

"Thanks, Mr. Duncan," she interrupted. "I'm glad we had this talk, but now I have to get to my first class." She turned and walked out of his room before he could say anything more.

She went to her locker to grab her textbooks, feeling more than a little ticked at Mr. Duncan. Okay, she'd failed one lousy test and missed a dumb appointment, but it wasn't as though she were a problem student who was always screwing up. He shouldn't have come down on her like that. Some teachers could be real hard-asses.

Across the hall, Gavin Colgan, a lowly grade-ten kid, was talking about the new hybrid electric cars. Zoë absently listened in.

"… and they're not only great for the environment because of reduced fuel emissions, but they're unbelievably quiet. Noise pollution is something we don't think much about, but we should. I'm betting hybrids are the wave of the future." Gavin's voice matched his body: thin and reedy.

Zoë agreed with the little guy. Everyone was concerned about exhaust fumes and carbon dioxide, but noise and light pollution shouldn't be ignored. She grabbed her binder from under a pile of extremely ripe gym clothes.

"You're so full of it, Colgan, always blabbing on like you know more than the rest of the world. You need to shut your mouth!"

Jarod Kaplinski, a tough kid with a big chip on his shoulder, and his three friends were standing around Gavin. Four-to-one odds, not good and not smart, Zoë decided.

Gavin bravely, or maybe foolishly, stood his ground. "I'm telling you, the cars of tomorrow will run on electricity, or maybe hydrogen fuel, and they'll be so quiet, rush hour will hardly be noticed."

Jarod backed Gavin up against the lockers and it didn't look good for the skinny kid.

Zoë slammed her door closed with a loud bang.

"He's right," she said, coming to Gavin's defence.

"Butt out of this, Kendall." Jarod threw Zoë a warning scowl before turning his attention back to the helpless Gavin.

Zoë's morning had already been a ten on the annoyance scale, and this little circus was not helping. Before she knew what she was doing, she'd moved between the two boys and was inches from Jarod's face.

"And another thing, Kaplinski." She glared at the bigger boy. "You should treat Gavin here a little nicer, because in a few years, you'll be working for him." She gave Jarod a push, sending him crashing into an open locker door. "Or maybe asking him if you can supersize his fries!"

Jarod roared and made a lunge at her.

Mr. Duncan stepped between Zoë and Jarod.

"Both of you, down to the office *now!*"

Zoë spent the next half-hour in the counsellor's office.

Chapter 10

Zoë's life had hit a wall. Everything she touched turned to garbage. Adam thought she'd practically lied to him, she was struggling at school, and now she had to tell her mother she was in trouble for fighting. Add to that the wicked nightmares she was having every night, and life sucked, big time.

When Zoë came home from school, she poked her head into the study to say hi to her mom. Her mother was dozing in her favourite chair, and with the golden afternoon light slanting through the tall windows, Zoë saw the worry etched on her face.

She didn't have the heart to disturb her. Silently, Zoë backed out of the room. Her mom had more than her share of trouble. It made Zoë want to make up for her brother's antics, to some-how fix things so at least one part of the Kendall saga didn't read like a traffic accident report.

Later that evening, Zoë was in her room doodling a design she'd had floating around in her head for a subtle new spoiler that would boost the downforce on a rally car without increasing drag and scrubbing off speed, like a wing did. A knock at her door interrupted her concentration.

"Zoë, honey, are you awake?"

Her mother's voice actually sounded excited, and if Zoë wasn't mistaken, happy. What could have changed from when she'd come home until now?

"Come on in, Mom."

"Sorry for missing dinner. I fell asleep and must have been out for the count." Her mother's glance fell on the empty potato-chip and cookie bags accompanied by several pop cans on Zoë's nightstand. "You should have woken me up. I could have fixed you something proper to eat."

Abruptly changing topics, her mother's expression lit up. "Guess what came in the mail today?"

"You secretly won the lotto and the cheque finally arrived?" Zoë raised her eyebrows.

"Better! Remember when you were worried about not having applied for your undergrad yet, and I told you everything would be okay?"

Her mother waited as impatiently as a kid in line for a ticket to the merry-go-round.

Zoë was getting a little nervous. "Yes …" she said slowly.

This was apparently the right answer, because her mother rushed ahead with her explanation.

"Well, the reason I knew you didn't need to worry was because I had already sent in your application for early admission. It's based on self-reported grades, and when I spoke to Mr. Duncan, he helped me with the details." She put a large brown envelope on Zoë's bed. "The registrar's office is being snippy and officious. Apparently I can't actually sign for you, so all you need to do is put your signature on the forms and return them ASAP. Isn't this exciting?"

Zoë was stunned. She didn't know what to say. She stared at the envelope feeling overwhelmed, not at her mother trying to enrol her without actually telling her — that was so like her mom that Zoë should have expected something like this. It was the whole reality check thing, and there was no doubt, this was a reality check, or maybe a wake-up call. It was really happening. Her future was here, sitting on her bed in a plain brown wrapper.

"Wow." Zoë took a deep breath. "Wow." She wished she could say something a little more profound, but for now, "Wow" was all she could come up with.

"I realize this is unexpected, but I know how you are with deadlines — so I thought I'd take that worry off your list. You can thank me later." Her mom gave her a quick hug as she rushed on. "This is so exciting. Oh, Zoë, I know you will do spectacularly. Right now, I'm feeling a little peckish. Do you want me to bring you something to eat — a salad perhaps, or maybe a piece of fruit?

Something in the main food groups besides fat and sugar?"

"No ... Ah, I'm fine thanks." Zoë was at a loss for words, and that didn't happen very often.

"Oh, and Zoë, my Mercedes is acting up. It's down on power and mysteriously surges when I try to accelerate. Your father said he'd deal with it, but of course, he didn't. I was hoping you might check it out."

Zoë ran the symptoms through her mind and then asked. "Mom, was there a gasoline tanker truck at the station when you last filled up?

Her mom pursed her lips as she thought about this. "Actually, there was. I had to wait to get to the pumps."

"I think your little SLK 350 has a plugged fuel filter."

"Oh, honey, that sounds serious. Maybe I should take it in to the shop."

"No need for that. Mom, this is what happened." Zoë held her notepad and quickly sketched the fuel filter cartridge and pump in the gas tank, then showed the path to how it fed into the injectors. "You picked up sludge stirred from the bottom of the gasoline storage tank after it was filled. I'll get the part, pull the trim panel off, open her up, and swap it out after school. No biggie."

"You can do that?"

"Yup, especially if I have your credit card to go to the parts department at the dealership!"

"I'll leave it on the table." Her mom inspected

the diagram of the spoiler on the page. "That's pretty. A school science project?"

"No, nothing important, just an idea I had." Zoë tossed the notepad onto the bed.

Her mother picked up the paper and studied the design. "This could be a part for a space-age super car. It seems very technical, like it was drawn by an …" Her eyes lifted from the page and locked with Zoë's. Something flashed across her face, then, with an adamant shake of her head, she dropped the notebook and left.

Alone again, Zoë was instantly drawn to the brown envelope. She felt mesmerised, as though it was a king cobra.

She should be thrilled. She should be dancing on the ceiling. She should be committed!

Instead, she opened the envelope and read the forms.

This was the big time. This was for keeps. This was what she and her mom had decided was the right thing to do. Zoë Kendall, MD.

But if this was the right thing, why wasn't she more excited? She thought of her mom's smiling face and realized she had enough excitement for the both of them.

Zoë took the pen from her backpack, and after reading the application, found another pen, one that didn't have pink ink. This was an adult decision and she wanted her signature to be adult. She signed her name in serious black ink.

Slipping the papers back into the envelope, Zoë

sealed it. Sealed, like her future, she thought. No more rallying, driving so fast light had trouble keeping up with her. Those days were over.

She leaned the envelope carefully against her dresser mirror, then beat on her homework. Her eyes kept straying to her dresser as though the envelope was a sea siren and she, a helpless sailor being lured to the rocks. When Zoë finally put her books away, she was exhausted.

Sleep evaded her even though she was dead tired. She'd almost doze off, then her eyes would pop open and she'd jerk wide awake, feeling anxious. In the moonlight, she could see the envelope sitting silently on her dresser.

**

It wasn't until she was on her way to school the next day that Zoë remembered the envelope. Overtired, she'd slept through her alarm, and in her hurry, had left the stupid thing on her dresser. She whipped a U-turn and sped back home. If she didn't mail that application, she'd never get any sleep.

Later, as she made her way to her locker, Zoë bumped into Kayla and they walked together.

"How's it going?"

Her friend's dress today was reminiscent of another age — the stone age. Lots of animal prints, and not-too-subtle bones dangling from her ears.

"Life is a blast," Kayla said with more than a

hint of sarcasm in her voice. "I was up till midnight working on my bio homework but I didn't get it finished. Mr. D is going to have a cow." She giggled. "Then he'll probably make me cut it up!"

Adam was at Zoë's locker when they arrived. Her heart skipped a beat, then sped up to make up for the one it had skipped.

"Can I talk to you for a minute?" He looked great in faded jeans and a black Champ Cars T-shirt.

"Sure, I have a minute." Zoë thought that sounded neutral enough that it couldn't possibly get her into trouble. One tiny part of her was worried he'd come to tell her he was breaking up, and if he had, she wanted to be able to act like it was cool with her. She gave an involuntary shiver at the thought. Kayla eyed Zoë and Adam, then tossed her books into her locker.

"Whoa! Too much goin' on here. Catch you later, girlfriend." She left, the bone earrings swinging gaily as she went.

"About the other day," Adam began awkwardly. "I, well, when you told me all our plans had changed, I guess I was pissed off. This is your life we're talking about, and if medicine's what you truly want, well then, go for it. I know you'll be a great doctor, Bunny."

She let out the breath she'd been secretly holding. "Yeah, we were both doing a lot of trash-talking, but I should have told you everything sooner. I messed up. I've been doing it a lot lately."

The crowded hallway faded away as they stared into each other's eyes, knowing there was more to say, but not wanting to damage the fragile truce between them.

Finally, Adam cleared his throat. "I was hoping you could come over tonight, after supper, around seven? If you're not too busy, that is."

Zoë wondered what was up, but knew better than to reject Adam when he was obviously holding out an olive branch. "I have a ton of homework, but sure, for an hour I guess."

"That's great. See you tonight!"

The twinkle in his eye made her spidey senses tingle. Something was definitely up.

As he walked away, Zoë pulled the U of C application out of her backpack and set it on the top shelf of her locker, so she'd remember to mail it after school.

Chapter 11

"I'm going over to Adam's tonight," Zoë told her mother as they dined alone again.

Her dad was still down east with Trent and Zoë wondered if the situation was so screwed up, even he couldn't straighten it out.

Her mother had been smiling since she'd come in from some errand she was being very secretive about, but when Zoë said this, her head came up sharply.

"Oh? And I suppose you're going to be working on that rally car of his." She pushed her plate back with a flick of her hand. "I thought that nonsense was all in the past, Zoë. Besides, I'm wondering if you might want to cancel on Adam when I tell you my news."

"He didn't say anything about working on the car, Mom. And I meant it when I said rallying is in the past, but I already told Adam I'd come over." Zoë glanced up as her mother's words finally registered.

"News? What news?"

Her mother's excitement was barely contained.

"Well, Zoë, this is the best thing that could have happened."

Her smile was back, which told Zoë it wasn't anything disastrous.

"If it's that good, you'd better not keep it a secret."

"Remember when you told me that the day of your unfortunate biology exam you had a migraine? When I heard that, it bothered me. You should never have written that exam under those circumstances."

Zoë was getting a little antsy. What had her mother done this time?

"Anyway, I went to Mr. Duncan and explained what had happened. I also took a note from your doctor stating that your headaches are completely debilitating, and that on the day you wrote the test, you did not have your proper medication."

"Mom, can you please cut to the chase?"

Her mother's hands fluttered like an excited bird's wings. "Certainly, dear. After long and serious discussion, Mr. Duncan has decided to let you rewrite the exam. He'll meet you at eight o'clock Saturday morning in the lab at school, and that mark is the one that will count. Isn't that the best news ever?"

Zoë was flabbergasted. It actually was great news! She'd felt like she was cheated on that lame exam. She could have passed easily if her brain hadn't been mush at the time.

"Mom, this is terrific!" She got up and hugged her mother, squeezing her hard enough for all the love Zoë felt to be absorbed. "Thank you, thank you, thank you! I don't know how you got Mr. D to agree, but what ever you did, you rock, Mom!"

Her mother blushed. "Oh, now stop that, Zoë. I hardly did anything at all."

Zoë vowed to ace the exam. She just needed to put in a little extra studying over the next couple of nights. Then she remembered Adam.

"Mom, I'm going to zip over to Adam's for an hour. I'll be back in plenty of time to hit the books, don't worry. I know I can pass that exam standing on my head, and I have tonight and tomorrow to study."

Zoë kissed her mom on the cheek and raced out the door.

***

After pulling into Adam's driveway, Zoë went straight to the garage in the back. She knew that's where he'd be.

"Knock-knock," she said when she saw his legs sticking out from under the red rally car. Man, that car looked fast standing still!

"Be right there, Zoë. Come on in." He was on a creeper, working at the front end of the Honda.

Zoë stopped and stared. The car was up on axle stands and both front and back ends were in various stages of being torn apart. The garage looked like a bomb had gone off in it.

Adam slid out from under the car and, standing, replaced some tools in the roller cabinet. She watched him for a moment. He had a tight little butt that could make even coveralls sexy.

He turned that boyish charm on and every cell in her body responded like flowers to the sun. The man was awesome! Zoë wondered what the odds were on successful long-distance romances? Maybe she and Adam could beat them after all.

"I have a surprise for you, actually two, and I think you're going to like it … ah … them!"

He winked at her and Zoë winked back. It was her day for surprises, she thought, as she followed Adam to a large tarp at the back of the garage.

"I know it's going to be tight to get these put in before Saturday, but I'm willing to give it a go if you are."

"What are you talking about?" Zoë was confused, and then Adam yanked the tarp off to reveal what was hidden beneath.

"Ta-dah!" He looked like a little boy who'd been given a pony of his very own.

Zoë stared at a large cardboard box marked "Gruber and Gruber Fabricators."

"Oh my gosh! They're here! No way!"

Adam was grinning from ear to ear. "Yes, Zoë, there is a Santa Claus!" He pulled the lid off the crate.

For Zoë, it really felt like Christmas.

The new suspension pieces were shiny and perfect. The custom-designed control arms and accompanying sway bars were nestled next to the new brackets and assorted bits to bolt the whole thing together.

Months ago, she'd sourced out complementing springs, shocks, and bushings, and they'd been waiting patiently in their boxes for her new trick control arms to arrive.

Zoë knelt beside the box and ran her fingers over the various pieces. "They're beautiful," she breathed, in a tone most teenaged girls reserve for a new Gucci handbag or a pair of Jimmy Choo heels. Her eyes lovingly caressed the parts, and then her mind took over.

"Where's the spec sheets? Do you have the original designs we sent? Where are my coveralls?"

They laid out the parts, checking each against the master sheet to make sure it was built exactly the way Zoë's designs had specified.

"That explains why you have the car torn to bits." She nodded toward the disassembled Civic.

"I thought I'd get a jump on things." He wiggled his eyebrows at her. "You can't blame me, can you?"

"I'd have done the same thing!"

As they unbolted the rear suspension, Zoë and Adam chatted amiably about the difference the new control arms would make to the handling of the car. Zoë had taken into account tons of vari-

ables, including weight transfer, body roll, suspension droop, and the type of handling she pre-
ferred from the car she piloted.

Before she knew it, three hours had sped by.
Zoë gasped when she checked her watch. She'd
been having such fun, she'd completely lost track
of the time.

"Oh man, my mom is going to kill me. I said
I'd be home hours ago. I've got to go, Adam."
Hurrying to the clothes rack, she wiggled out of
her coveralls.

Adam wiped his hands on a rag. "No worries.
It's time to pack it in for tonight anyway. This was
one productive night. We got a lot done."

There were parts spread over every flat surface.
"It might take an all-nighter, but we can finish
bolting everything in tomorrow, and it will be
ready to fly bright and early Saturday. We are
going to kick butt at the rally, Bunny. I can hardly
wait."

Zoë's breath caught in her throat. Saturday was
the rally! With everything else going on, it had
slipped her mind. She remembered Mr. Duncan
and the makeup exam and her heart sank. Her
mom had gone to so much trouble to arrange
everything, and Zoë had said once that application
was mailed …

"Damn!" She slapped her forehead. The application was still in her locker at school! She'd forgotten it again.

Adam looked at her questioningly.

"I was supposed to mail something." Well, it was as good as mailed, and that meant her new life path was already started.

She had to make the break as clean and as painless as possible.

"Adam, I can't drive in the rally on Saturday. When I said I wasn't going to spend so much time with cars and rallying, I meant it. I have to concentrate on my future in medicine. In fact, that bio exam I failed so miserably, I get to rewrite it Saturday morning, and that will really help my overall mark."

His face showed disappointment, then something she hadn't expected — anger.

"You're kidding right?" he said. His voice had that sharp edge she recognized from the few times she'd seen him really furious. When his temper did show, she was always glad it wasn't directed at her.

"No, Adam. The rewrite is all arranged."

He walked over to the bench and put the wrench he'd been holding back into the toolbox. When he turned to her, Zoë could see his jaw muscles were tight.

"We've been entered in this rally for months, and I thought it was important to both of us. But since I only got the bulletin about your new game plan a couple of days ago, I didn't realize that meant everything we've worked for was cancelled."

Zoë didn't like Adam's tone. "I tried to tell you

that my plans have gone in a different direction. I thought you understood."

"What I understand is this — it's Thursday night. The rally is two days away. I will not be able to find a replacement driver in time, which means I can't compete either. It's a *team* competition Zoë — a driver and a co-driver, you and me. If you're out, I'm out."

"I'm sorry Adam, but I've made up my mind." Zoë felt her throat tightening and she knew she had to leave. She turned and ran from the garage.

Chapter 12

Zoë lay awake that night thinking about Adam. What she'd done to Adam sucked, but everything was happening so fast, the rally had sort of crept up on her. And there was that big promise she'd given her mom hanging in the air — Zoë Kendall and cars were done.

But she also knew Adam was right. He'd never be able to find a replacement driver in so short a time. His race was over before it had begun. She couldn't have done a worse thing to him if she'd tried.

She closed her eyes. *Go to sleep, go to sleep, go to sleep*, she repeated in her head like a mantra.

Crap! She sat bolt upright.

The application in the top of her locker! This was *redonculous*, to use Kayla's improvised word for *too stupid to believe*. She couldn't forget it again. Hopping out of bed, Zoë fumbled in her backpack for a package of sticky notes.

Scribbling herself a reminder, she stuck it to the outside of her backpack. *MAIL APPLICATION!* Then she climbed back into bed.

He mind went straight to Adam and the rally. *No! Stop thinking about it!* That was now officially in the past. She threw the covers back and got up again. Writing herself another note, she went to her bathroom and stuck this one in the middle of the mirror. *MAIL APPLICATION, DUMMY!* She clambered back into bed, but still couldn't sleep.

Kicking the blankets off, she got up and grabbed the sticky notes, a pen, and put her slippers on before heading downstairs. She put another note on the fridge, then the back door, and finally, she went out to her car and stuck one on the dash. *MAIL APPLICATION OR THE WORLD WILL END!*

Tired and cold, she padded back up to her room and fell into bed. Tomorrow, right after school, she'd march into the post office and mail that sucker.

***

The next day went by in a fog. Zoë was exhausted and had serious trouble focusing. Miracle of miracles, she did remember to take her application out of her locker. But she'd been late getting away from school and by the time she'd raced to the door of the post office at the mall, it was closed.

She stuffed the annoying envelope into her backpack. It would have to wait till Monday now. Maybe she could send it Super Fast Express Delivery, or some other expensive way to make up for being such a dolt about it all week.

***

When Zoë got home after school Friday, her mom had left a note saying she'd gone out for groceries and would be back later.

Zoë grabbed a snack and spent the evening studying for the big exam. Without the pounding screamer of a migraine, everything made sense, and the answers came easily. She felt good about tomorrow. In fact, she actually felt confident.

Then Zoë thought of Adam, and her heart sank. She'd ruined things with him forever, that much she was sure of. And she'd been thinking they could continue their relationship on a long-distance basis. Ha! She couldn't keep the two of them going when they were only a few blocks away from each other, let alone thousands of kilometres.

There was a knock on her bedroom door.

"Honey, I brought you something to eat." Home from shopping and in full Mother Mode, her mom bustled into Zoë's room with a plate of sandwiches, a granola bar, and a tall iced tea.

"Thanks. I don't know what I'd do without you." Zoë smiled as her mom set the tray down on the bedside table.

"I only want what's best for my little girl, and studying on an empty stomach isn't good." She sat on the edge of the bed. "Are you sleeping all right, sweetheart? You seem a little frazzled."

"Oh, maybe a little overextended. But nothing I can't handle." Zoë wasn't about to tell her mom about ruining Adam's rally, or how she'd blown their life plans out of the water. She also didn't want to mention her nightmares, now that Trent, with all his problems, was screaming for attention.

"I have some news. I talked to your father today. Trent is going to take a semester off from his studies and come home for a while. It seems he's having trouble finding himself and needs to think things over. They're flying in tonight."

Zoë looked up quickly. "Trent's coming home?" She thought about her brother, with his bad track record and ADHD. This news did nothing to lighten Zoë's mood. Trent back home after getting tossed from McGill was not going to make for a lot of warm fuzzies around the Kendall household.

She blinked and rubbed the sudden tension in her forehead. On top of all this, her dad still hadn't heard anything about her new career direction. The steel band squeezing her head cranked a little tighter.

She boiled when she thought about Trent — man, he was a real treat!

Then it struck her what it must be like for her big brother. From her own gross recent experiences, she knew being a teenager was a tough job, even for someone with no clinical problems. A light went on in Zoë's brain. She now understood why her parents paid such huge attention to Trent. He was damaged, and needed more tolerance and guidance than she ever had. In a way, her parents not hovering over her had been a compliment. It meant they thought she could handle things on her own.

And she had, until her mom decided coasting wasn't the best way of handling things. She hadn't known about Zoë's engineering plans, so it made sense the mother radar would kick in and focus on Zoë eventually.

Sure, Trent was supposed to be grown up now. But maybe growing up wasn't a straight line; maybe we occasionally slid backward and needed our parents to step in. Sometimes, life was overwhelming, and it was nice to let mom and dad take over while the kid in us caught our breath.

Her mother ran her fingers along the quilted edge of Zoë's bedspread in much the same way her daughter did when she was stalling for time.

"Honey, there's something else I want to talk to you about. Your father and I also discussed a lot of other things today." Her mother sounded nervous. "Our long-distance bill is going to be a doozy this month." She cleared her throat self-consciously.

"You don't know this Zoë, but your father and I have been going through ... a little rough patch."

Zoë saw how hard this was for her mother to

talk about. She didn't mention she'd already figured there was trouble in paradise.

A terrible tightening in her throat made Zoë realize she was afraid of what her mother was going to say next. Was she going to tell Zoë they were getting a divorce? That would be the absolute worst. No way did she want her parents to split. She held her breath.

"Anyway, your father and I talked it over and we've decided to go to a marriage counsellor to try and work things out. I want you to know that we love each other very much, but lately, we've been drifting. Sometimes in a marriage, that happens. It's no one's fault, or maybe it's both our faults. We want to stop that drifting trend and get things back the way they were."

Something changed in her expression, and Zoë felt like they'd suddenly become equals — not mother and daughter, but friends confiding to one another.

Her mother went on in a quiet voice. "I want to give you a piece of advice that I hope, if you're ever serious about someone, you'll remember. Zoë, a relationship is a living thing — it needs nurturing and care, or it will wither and die. Caring for the one you love is hard work, and it doesn't stop because you get married or are living together. In fact, that's when you should try your hardest. The person you're dating, the one who is always trying to please, will not be the same person once you're married. You'll discover he has a lot of annoying traits you never noticed before. What you have to remember is that you won't be the same person, either, you'll reveal your own flaws. We all have them. So you both need to remember the person you fell in love with is the same person leaving his socks lying around and the cap off the toothpaste."

Zoë laid her hand on her mother's arm. "That's the best advice you've ever given me, and I won't forget. I promise. And I'm really glad to hear you and Dad are going to work on things, Mom."

"Keep in mind, this is girl talk, Zoë, and we'll keep it between the two of us. When your father and Trent come home, we won't mention a word." She covered her daughter's hand with hers. "It's great to have someone to talk to, sweetheart. Oh, and I got an email from the head of my old sorority chapter. You are definitely going to be fast-tracked. I'd say your life has moved to another level."

She stood up. "And now, young lady, back to the books. I know you'll do brilliantly tomorrow."

"There's no cow eyeball or fish intestines that I can't handle!" Zoë grinned.

Wow, the universe had cranked it up a notch! Trent was coming home and this time, Zoë felt like she was the big sister, and not the least bit intimidated by her older brother. Her parents were going to work on their relationship, and that took a big weight off Zoë. Why she felt this way she didn't know, but it was like a cloud was lifting.

Her life path was mapped out and very rosy, and now her parents were going to be fine. Yup, things were moving along. Then why did she feel like she'd lost her best friend and was being marched off to a prison camp?

She should be happy. But deep down, she still felt like she was red-lining her life and heading for a cliff.

***

That night, the car in her dream was different. It was still going to get creamed by a semi-trailer heading straight for it, but this time, Zoë was behind the wheel. The big truck careened straight for her, but at the last second, Zoë cranked the wheel, deftly avoiding the big rig. The innovatively designed car handled beautifully. In the surreal dream landscape, it was as if the car responded to her very thoughts, without her having to do a thing. She hammered on the brakes. The ABS shuddered a complaint, but the car remained in her control. A crowd standing at the side of the road cheered. Zoë climbed out of the car and realized why they were cheering. On the door was written: *Improved Safety Handling Designed by Zoë Kendall, P.Eng.*

When she awoke, she was smiling.

Chapter 13

Zoë dressed carefully, tugging on her lucky jeans. She was sure she'd pass, but a little insurance never hurt. Grabbing her backpack with the application envelope sticking guiltily out of the top, she dragged her butt downstairs. She kept telling herself it was *exam day, exam day,* but a small insistent bell at the back of her brain chimed, *No way, it's rally day*!

Zoë's dad and Trent were already at the table eating stacks of pumpkin pancakes when she walked in. She tossed her backpack toward her chair, where it fell unceremoniously to the floor. "Hey, you two! Welcome home!" She turned on a thousand-watt smile, mostly for her father.

Zoë's dad got up to give her a big bear hug. "Hello, princess. It's great to be back with my two best girls." He held her close. "I hear you have a test today. I know you'll knock 'em dead."

Zoë wiggled out of her dad's embrace. "Thanks for the vote of confidence."

"Your mother outdid herself. We feast today. I suggest you tuck in before your brother has fourths."

Turning to her brother, Zoë noted the downcast eyes and the stiff posture.

"Hey, Trent. How's it goin'?" she asked brightly.

Her brother shrugged, not bothering to look up as he lavished syrup on his packed-to-capacity plate. "It's been better. But I'm home now, in the warm bosom of my family."

Zoë was instantly stung. This was the old obnoxious Trent, before he was diagnosed with ADHD and put on Ritalin. There was only one thing that could make him revert to his caveman persona, and it would account for his trouble at school, too.

Zoë suspected Trent had stopped taking his medication.

Her heart pounded. She'd seen what happened when Trent turned on his "charm." They'd all be at each other's throats in no time. She sat next to her brother.

Trent went on, as though talking to himself. "I take a few days off, mental stress days I call them, and all hell breaks loose. Honestly, those clowns at McGill have no idea what I go through."

Zoë decided to find out if what she suspected was true.

"Maybe the clowns don't understand. Maybe you should tell them you need special consideration because of your ADHD. You know, show them your medication and explain." She sounded very sincere.

Trent shook his head agitatedly, then leaned in and whispered so only she could hear. "They say I need to keep taking all those damn chemicals to flatten me out, but I decided they should get to know the real genius hiding behind the drugs."

He held his finger up to his lips; his eyes were fever bright. "Don't let dear old Mom and Pops know."

Bingo! He was off his Ritalin. How was she going to get him to take his meds without telling her parents? Her brain kicked into high-stress overdrive as her brother continued his rant.

"I can pass their stupid exams without cracking a book. That's what freaks them. I'm smarter than half those professors, and they know it."

Zoë was not surprised he didn't think to ask her how her life was going. Same old Trent, the universe revolved around him. The problem was, he could be a real sweet guy when he was on his Ritalin. She felt a little dizzy. What could she do? Whatever it was, she had to do it fast. Her parents would figure out what was going on in a heartbeat, and then everyone's crazy levels would go through the roof. And what would that do to her mom and dad's plans for reconciliation?

Her mother set a plate down in front of Zoë, startling her out of her reverie. "Good morning, sweetheart. Ready for your big exam?"

Zoë's stomach did a backflip. Eating was the last thing she wanted to do. She swallowed as she stared down at four slimy eggs sliding around on the plate.

Her mother seemed oblivious to Zoë's discomfort as she bustled about. "I made pancakes for the boys, and for you, soft poached eggs — protein for the exam, and circle toast," she laughed. "Do you remember calling bagels that when you were a little girl?"

As Zoë's mom joined the rest of the family with her own plate of food, she didn't notice the backpack sticking out from beneath the chair.

"Oops!" The food shifted dangerously, then the coefficient of friction succumbed to the force of gravity, and the eggs, sausages, hash browns, and two orange slices slid off the plate and onto Zoë's lap.

Zoë's upset stomach climbed into her throat as the jumbled mess soaked into her lucky jeans.

"Oh ... my ... Gawd!"

Trent snickered loudly.

"Oh no! Honey, I'm so sorry!" her mother apologized. Her eyes then fell on the offending backpack peeking out from under Zoë's chair.

Zoë followed her mother's gaze to the brown envelope sticking out of the top.

"Zoë, is this your U of C application we filled out days ago?" Her mother retrieved the envelope. "Why on earth haven't you mailed it yet?"

Her father's head came up. "What application?"

"I can explain, Mom." Zoë ignored her dad for the moment — one calamity at a time. "I sort of kept forgetting to mail it, and then when I remembered, the post office was closed. I plan on mailing it Monday for sure."

"It seems odd that you would forget something so important ..." Her mother frowned.

Zoë had to agree. Why had she continually forgotten it?

She read the sticky note stuck to the front and blanched. She'd made a mistake when she'd scribbled the note. She thought she'd written: *Mail Application or the World Will End*. What it actually said was, *Mail Application and the World Will End*. Zoë shivered at the brutal truth.

"Will someone tell me what's going on?" her father asked again.

Zoë turned to her dad. "The condensed version goes like this: I've decided to go to U of C and get a degree in medicine. This means giving up other things, like rallying and cars, but I'm totally okay with it."

Her father hesitated. "I thought you were heading in another direction, Zoë. Didn't you want to continue working with cars in a professional capacity — like automotive engineering and design?"

How he'd known this, Zoë couldn't figure out, unless her dad was way more attentive than she'd thought. Maybe he'd been listening to her all these years after all.

"I know, Daddy, but Mom and I talked about it and we think medicine is right for me."

Her father looked from Zoë to her mom sceptically.

Her mother's chin lifted a notch in defiance, a gesture Zoë recognized as one she used herself.

"Steven, she needs a future with promise. Medicine will give her that."

His brows furrowed. "I think engineering would give her the same thing, Laura. I'm questioning your decision because she's never shown any interest in medicine before. I had no idea she was bored with cars."

Zoë jumped in. "I'm not bored with cars, Dad."

"No more cars!" her mother interjected.

Trent suddenly waved his pancake-laden fork toward them.

"You should all chill! Will you listen to yourselves, arguing over whether little sister here goes into medicine or engineering? For crying out loud, she could make worse choices, like being a bag lady or running a crack house."

Zoë smiled at her big brother for the first time that morning. "Thanks, Bro."

"Stop playing the devil's advocate, Trent, this is serious," Zoë's mother snapped.

"Mom, he's right!" Zoë said, defending her brother.

"What a gong show!" Trent guffawed as he stuffed the dangling pancakes into his mouth.

"Now princess," Zoë's dad went on, "I can understand your mother's point. She's right. You deserve a future with success. I love rallying too, but I make my money as a litigator. What field of medicine will you specialise in?"

Zoë couldn't keep up. She felt dizzy.

At that moment, the doorbell rang, as though signalling the end of round one.

Chapter 14

"I'll get it!"

Saved by the doorbell, Zoë sighed as she grabbed a dishcloth to wipe her gooey hands.

"For crying out loud!" Trent grumbled. "What kind of a loony bin is this?"

Zoë opened the door and stared, speechless.

"Can I come in for a minute?" Adam asked quietly.

"Ah, sure." She stood back and let him in.

Adam looked surprised to see the whole family assembled. "Hi Mr. Kendall. Hey, Trent, buddy, welcome home."

Trent nodded. "Yeah, I decided to give you bunch a treat and stop by for a month or two."

"Great, we'll get together and play catch-up." Adam turned back to Zoë. "I came here to tell you something and although it might not be the right time ..." He checked out her greasy jeans. "Here goes anyway. The other night, I was out of line. You said you were backing off from rallying, and I should have asked then what this meant for our team. I guess I thought if I didn't ask, you couldn't say we were finished — the team, that is."

Zoë didn't know what to say. Her life was already way too complicated.

"I have to write an exam this morning," she whispered. "My bio makeup test. Mom arranged it with Mr. D."

Adam took a step toward her. "After everything went down the tubes, I forgot to give you the other surprise I had." He reached into his pocket and took out a white envelope then handed it to her.

The return address was *University of Ontario*.

Adam went on. "It's your application to the faculty of engineering. I requested one for both of us, but I guess after what you told me, it's meaningless. The thing is, *you* have to throw it out, Zoë. I can't. I know how much being an automotive engineer means to you."

Zoë's hands started to shake. Adam's face held all the sadness in the world, and perhaps even, resignation. It was as though he'd closed the very door she'd been trying to shut for weeks now.

"I, I don't know what to say."

Zoë swiped at her face, then stared down at the tear on her fingertip. It was so clear, like a tiny prism.

Trent stood up with a noisy scrape of his chair. "It seems little sister has a dilemma"

"What's this all about?" her mother demanded.

"Engineering's out of the question now, Adam," her dad said. "Zoë's settled on medicine."

"And the circus continues!" Trent tossed the empty fork he'd been holding onto the table, leaving a syrup imprint on the tablecloth.

Zoë wished they'd all be quiet so she could hear herself think.

She looked at her mom, then her dad, and finally her brother, willing herself to be calm. All the years of biting her tongue whenever there was a family meltdown was rising up in front of her. Trent grinned at her devilishly, and Zoë could have smacked him for messing up again. He knew he had to take his Ritalin, and he'd chosen to stop it. It wasn't her responsibility to keep peace in the family while Trent figured out what to do with his life.

"Trent, you need to shut up now," she said. "You're off your meds and are behaving like an ass. A couple of minutes ago, I was all set to start babysitting you again, but I think I'll take a piece of advice I gave Mom a while ago and cut the cord."

She shot him the no-nonsense look her dad used in the courtroom. "Sit down and stay out of this. You have your own problems to work on."

Her brother opened his mouth to say something. Clearly, he was not used to his baby sister putting him in his place.

"Oh Zoë, honey," said her mom before Trent could answer. "That's no way to speak to your brother. Have some patience."

Zoë had heard that speech a hundred times, and like clockwork, her dad jumped in.

"Laura, Trent was out of line and should step back."

Her mother's voice went up a notch. "Steven, these two children have got to get along, and Zoë knows Trent's medical problems should never be thrown in his face."

Zoë clamped her hands over her ears. She felt like she was in the eye of a hurricane. Everything was about to blow apart.

She searched the room for a lifebuoy, and her gaze fell on Adam. He held her gaze, strength flowing from him to her.

A sudden calmness came over Zoë. She was tired. She'd been in this pattern her whole life. Trent would mess up, and she'd try to make it better. She didn't want her family to fight, so if that meant giving in on everything, she did, the same way she'd given in to her mom about becoming a doctor.

There was only one problem — it was destroying her.

She remembered her dream from last night. Her nightmares had been trying to tell her something, but not what she'd assumed. The message wasn't that she *shouldn't* design cars, but that she absolutely had to. She was sure now that, one day, she'd design a feature in a car that would save lives, maybe even her own.

Her subconscious had been plotting against her,

making her forget to mail the U of C application, just as her dreams had shown her that she should go on with her goal of designing the world's best cars.

In an instant of total clarity, everything made sense. She couldn't live this lie anymore. Trying to please everyone, giving away her soul — she had to make that stop, she had to take control.

"I promised Mom I was through with cars, but saying it and believing it are two different things. You all have to trust me; I do want to design cars. I dream of designing cars — literally!"

Zoë reached a tentative hand toward Adam, then self-consciously drew it back. "And I want to be with you."

"I'm sorry, Mom, " she said firmly. "I can't go through with medical school. The price is too steep." A question occurred to Zoë. "A long time ago, you told me you had a dream for your own future. What was it?"

Her mother appeared confused for a moment. "Why, I dreamed of becoming a doctor, of course." She stopped; understanding lit up her eyes as she walked slowly over to her daughter. "But now I understand something I should have seen a long time ago. It's my dream that's finally over."

It took Zoë a moment for her mother's words to sink in.

"The truth is, Dad's right. I have zero interest in medicine. I want to design beautiful automobiles.

Mom, that's my dream, and I'm going to work hard to make it come true."

Her mom took the white envelope from the University of Ontario out of Zoë's trembling hand and turned to Adam, brandishing the letter like a sword.

"This is all your doing, Adam Harlow."

Then her mother did an unexpected thing. She smiled. "And I see now that it's a very good thing you stepped in."

She took the U of C application she was holding and, with a flourish, ripped it in two.

"Zoë, I don't think you'll be needing this after all."

Zoë stared at her mother. The morning light shone on her lovely face, and for the first time, Zoë noticed the fine lines around her mom's blue eyes. She also saw the silver among the gold of her perfectly arranged hair. Zoë had never thought of her mother growing old, but now, she saw time was passing for all of them.

There was acceptance in her mother's voice when she spoke.

"Honey, when I saw you hadn't made any plans for your future, I guess I thought I could live my dream through you. When you mentioned designing cars, I didn't want to believe how important it was to you. Instead, I dismissed it as childish, and went full steam ahead with my own ideas on what you should do."

Her eyes flickered to Trent. "Maybe deep

down, I thought if I couldn't help my ADHD son by being a doctor, then you could as his MD sister. I was wrong."

She rolled her eyes. "I remember when you were little and played race-car driver with your brother. You'd carefully draw the engine on the cardboard box and were very particular what colour of crayon was used for each part. I guess I couldn't see the forest for the trees, like the way I ignored that car design you were working on in your room.

Then she turned back to Adam. "I owe you a big thank-you — for not giving up, for coming here this morning and making both of us see things the way they really are. I guess Zoë does have the Kendall car gene and I was trying to fight Mother Nature."

Trent sat silently watching, and when Zoë saw him, her anger evaporated. Her brother looked lost and, surprisingly, very young. She knew she'd keep helping him, even if it annoyed the heck out of her. That's what sisters did. She grinned at Trent, and he gave her a weak smile back.

Zoë felt since she was clearing the air, she may as well continue: "Adam, I want to tell you again how sorry I am I screwed up the rally today. I left you with a dismantled car and an empty driver's seat, not to mention forfeiting our entry fee."

"Ah, actually, Bunny, the car is a runner. I was so upset on Thursday that I stayed up all night and bolted in the new suspension, then I tested it out yesterday, and it is sweet."

Zoë's mind was racing. If only she didn't have to write that stupid exam. It hit her like a bolt from the blue. Kayla had said this was test number six and that only the four highest scores counted! She had a passing mark now — not as high as it could be, but a pass for sure. She could ditch this exam!

"Adam ... what time is the first stage?"

"First car out is at nine."

"If we left right now, we could pick up that shiny little rally car, beg for a late tech inspection, and still be in time for the first stage."

She turned to her mother. "Mom, I'm not going to write that exam," she said. "I'll call Mr. D and tell him I've been abducted by aliens or something and I'll face the music on Monday."

Zoë was excited now. She went to Adam and kissed him. She'd never kissed Adam in front of her family before, and he blushed furiously, but she noticed he kissed her back. She stole a peek at her mother, not sure how she would take all of this.

Laura Kendall's arm was around her husband's waist and she gave him a little squeeze.

"Here's a deal I think you'll like, sweetheart. You make me a proud rally mom, and your dad and I will make your excuses to Mr. Duncan. She looked up at her husband. "What do you think, counsellor. Can we win this case?"

Steven Kendall smiled at his wife. "I think,

together, we can make a damn convincing argument,"

Zoë knew now everything was going to be okay. She was closer to her mom than she had ever been before and she liked the feeling. It was a feeling based on honesty.

"Hey Mom, do you think Delta Kappa Phi has a chapter at the University of Ontario?"

Her mother laughed. "We'll find out later. Right now, you and Adam have a rally to win."

Epilogue

The rally was fierce. Every competitor was going for the gold, and the newly reunited team of Kendall and Harlow was no exception.

"The new suspension rocks!" Zoë yelled into her mic as the Honda Civic flew around a corner.

They were on the final stage of the rally and everything had gone perfectly. The adrenaline in her system made her ears hum and Zoë loved it.

"Straight, forty metres, three left!" Adam called back, reading the pace notes that guided Zoë as she made her lightning-fast turns and bullet sprints on the straights.

A good co-driver could make or break a win. Adam was the best, and Zoë knew it.

"This is unbelievable! I never thought I'd be doing this again!"

She laughed as she geared down and took the

tight corner, clipping the apex at exactly the right point.

"Straight, one hundred metres, hairpin right," Adam sang out.

Zoë felt a tingling rush. God, she loved it when he talked to her like that!

A large cobble rumbled ominously off the skid plate. She checked her oil pressure gauge. Everything was still a go.

The car flew down the straight. Zoë braked and headed into the hairpin. Too late, she realized the corner was off-camber. She tried to compensate, but the inside of the curve where she'd planned her new apex was washed out. There wasn't enough room for her alternate racing line, and the car started to slide wide.

Zoë knew what was coming and it wasn't good. In a heartbeat, the race had turned deadly.

"Hold on, Adam. We're going bushwhacking!"

She straightened the wheels and hit the edge of the embankment at exactly the right angle to prevent a rollover. There was no time to be frightened. She had her hands full keeping the car from flipping.

Somewhere in the back of her mind, she wondered if this was what it had been like for Trent when he'd crashed his car. She would hug her brother as soon as she got home.

Hurtling down the steep incline, Zoë struggled to control the car as she weighed all her options. That was easy — she had none. All she could do was ride this out and try to keep them both alive.

Gently pumping the brakes, she was able to steer around a tree that suddenly jumped into their path.

"Crap!" she yelled, narrowly skirting a jagged boulder that had appeared out of nowhere. With a bone-jarring bang, the car came to rest at the bottom of the ravine.

A dust cloud enveloped the Honda as Zoë hit the starter trying to fire up the stalled car. Maybe she could drive it out of this ugly gully and get them back into the rally before they'd lost too much time.

The starter turned over, but the engine didn't catch.

Adam hit the release on his safety harness. "Hold on. I'll see if I can spot the problem."

He was out of the car and pulling the hood pins in a blink of an eye. After a quick check of the engine compartment, he leaned down and peered under the car. Seconds dragged by on crutches. Zoë could hear her raspy breathing inside her helmet. This was not the way the rally was supposed to go. They were supposed to win! It was her day.

"I'm afraid the intrepid team of Harlow and Kendall …" Adam began, straightening up and dusting off his Nomex driving suit.

"… *Kendall* and Harlow," she corrected, as she undid her own harness. She already knew what Adam was going to say, and it sucked, big time.

"Okay, the intrepid team of Kendall and Harlow will DNF today, due to a crushed exhaust pipe. I don't know what you hit, Bunny, but you smacked something hard enough to bend the skid plate." Adam closed the hood and pulled off his helmet. "This baby isn't going anywhere. We're walking back to the service area for a tow."

"*Did Not Finish!* My dad will be bummed, and you know something? I think my mom will be too."

Zoë climbed out of the car with a sigh. "It was fun while it lasted." She pulled off her helmet, then patted the hood of their broken car. "Don't worry, old girl. We'll be back for you later."

Adam took her hand as they climbed the embankment and started walking, careful to stay off the road. The next car sped by them a minute later, blasting its horn as the co-driver gave Zoë and Adam a quick wave through the passenger window.

Zoë grinned and waved back. "The Dixons seem particularly pleased with our little exhaust problem."

"In our class, we were definitely the team to beat," Adam said with a smile.

"We *are* the team to beat," Zoë corrected. "We'll be back. My new suspension is too sweet to sit in a garage for long."

"I can't argue with you on that one. You did a great job." Adam gave her a quick kiss.

"You put the whole thing together and tweaked it perfectly," Zoë said, slipping her arm around his waist.

The early summer smells of sun-warmed grass and clear mountain air made her feel she could soar into the bright sunshine like a butterfly on a breeze. She'd have a tough time deciding if this was the sweetest dream ever, or whether she was, in fact, totally awake.

"Hey, I've been thinking."

"Mmmm," Adam said.

"Do you leave your socks lying around, or the cap off the toothpaste by any chance?"

He raised his eyebrows.

"I mean, since we're both going to be down east, maybe we should think about being room-mates when we're finished our degrees. I heard it's expensive to live in Toronto, and it might help with the cash flow if we shared an apartment."

"You're so practical, Zoë Kendall. It makes perfect sense to me." Adam grabbed her around the waist and swung her in a circle. "I'll check if that position's been filled."

Zoë wrapped her arms around his neck and laughed as she held on tightly.

"Oh, it's filled, Adam Harlow, no doubt about it. It's filled!"